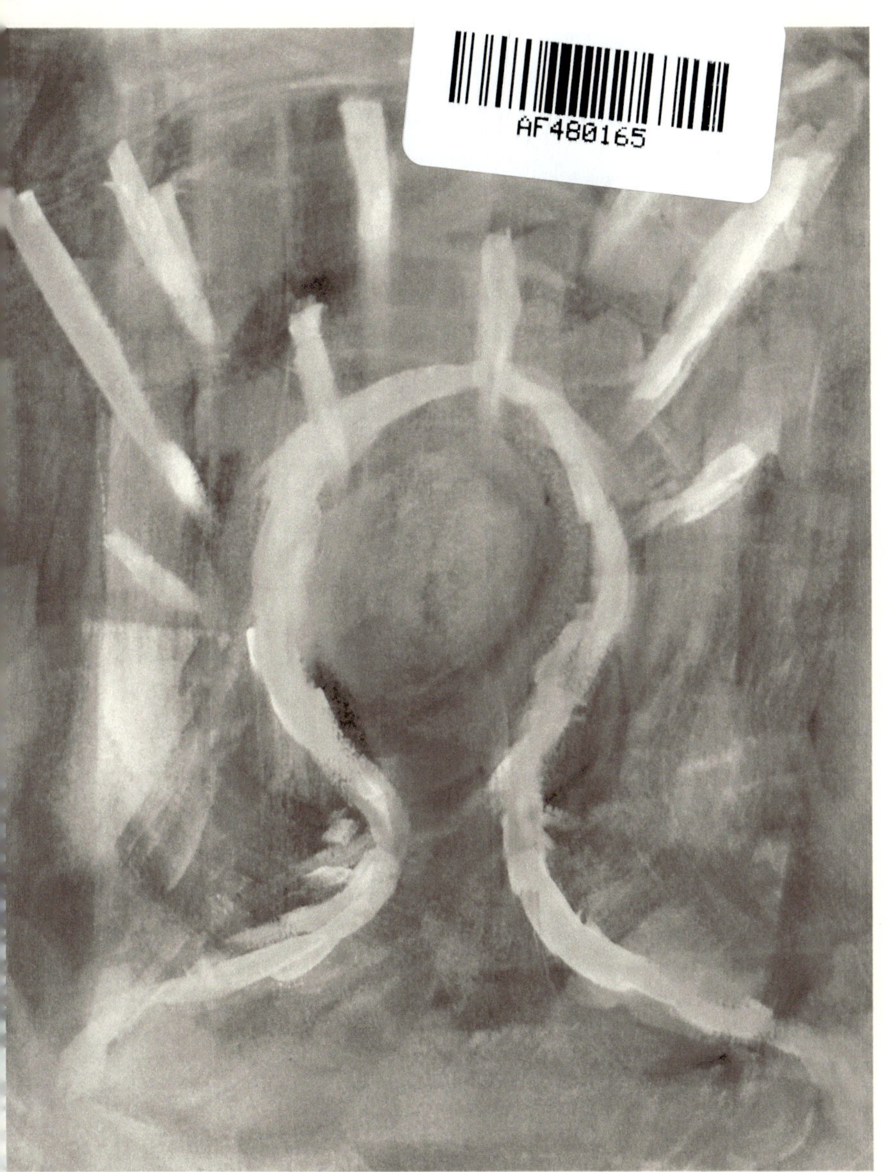

KARTAVYAM

ONUS UPON US by PAREEKSHITH REDDY

The journey of an individual may differ but the goal shall remain to be, to be True to oneself and not be carried away by fantasies. This fictional story is a commentary of a person's journey by his inner voice, in the third person. The goal of the inner voice is to reach a stage where there is nothing another person can tell them about themselves that they don't already know. Acquiring Knowledge is Life's Treasure and Wise living its Pleasure. It is an impossible goal. This is the pursuit of an Inner Voice at this very goal.

COVER PAGE ARTWORK

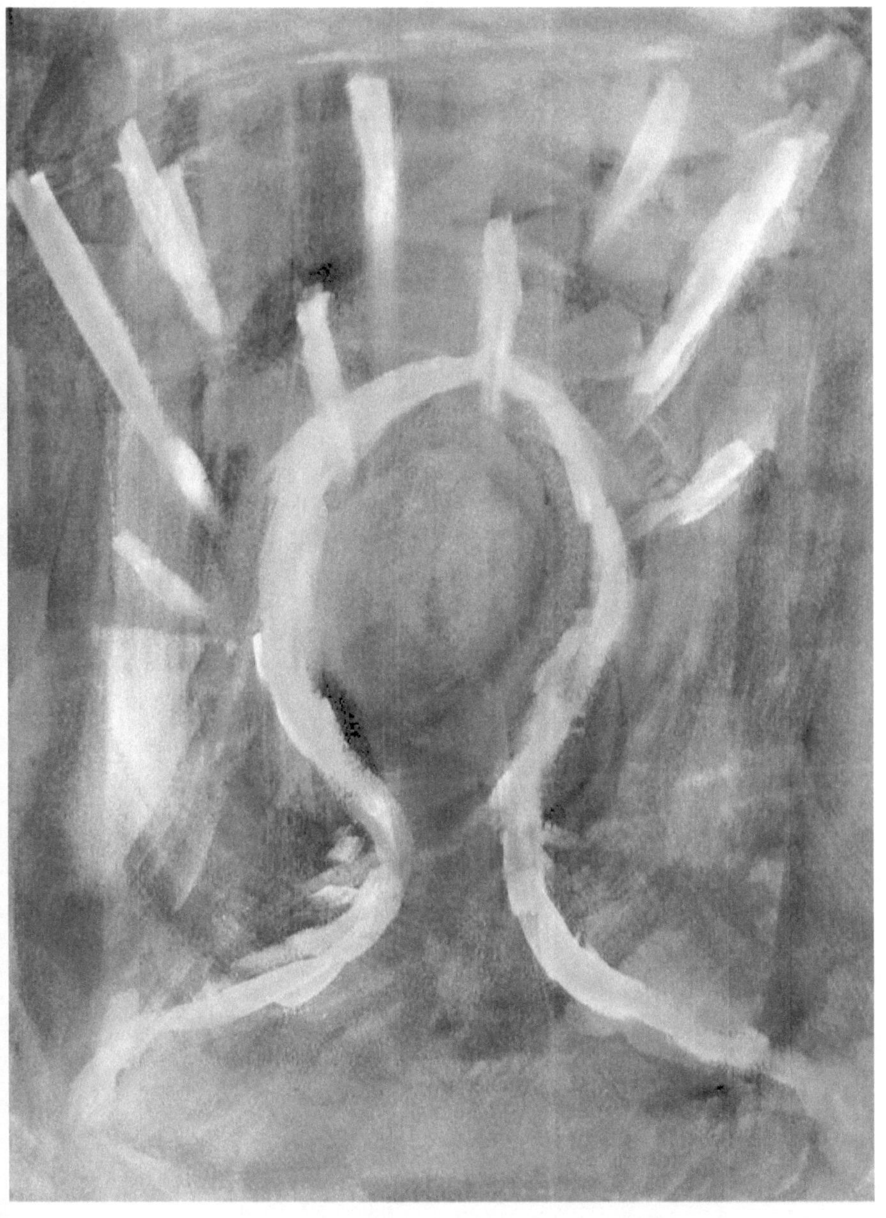

Title: Realize - Cover Page Art Work by Pareekshith Reddy

The Image on the Cover page of this book is an Art work by the Author, titled "Realise". It's a conceptual art which may be considered as Modern Cubism. Conceptual Art in this case is accompanied by the Artist's story associated with the painting. Thus conveying the depth in both Visual and Audible components. The viewer is further encouraged to use their own imagination to come up with their own and even better interpretations of the Art work.

Concept for Realise, the Art work, started off with an idea that our Minds start off as a blank white page. Upon the blank page, some from observations and others from pure inspiration, there are all sorts of thoughts that are occupying the mind. To capture each thought, the artist has used a different colour or a combination of Colours. With all different compartments and degrees of complexities, the page filled with colourful thoughts is how our mind can be imagined to be.

From all the various thoughts and ideas in one's mind, a personality develops, from within which a person manifests himself. It captures the moment of Realisation that one's thoughts and ideas are what makes a Mind. What occupies the mind becomes the mind, realising yourself in it shows you what you may become. If not the whole thing, you may at least see an outline of it.

Author's Note

The reason for the quick read format is because I already know that we're too busy. I didn't want to become the problem I'm trying to solve, the problem of distraction. It's a quick read, but is not an easy one. Don't read it trying to find a problem with the book, read as if you are trying to find a solution to your life in it. Like with everything else in life, things are not going to be handed to you. This is an effort by the author to present the reader with the next best thing to it, 49 different chapters describing at least 49 different facets to help with realising your Kartavyam. Be hawk-eyed, you might end up finding yourself in it.

It must be beyond discussion that all the good that people get, except Children, must be earned. I retired early and absolutely hated every day since, being fully at peace. If that's not living to the fullest, I don't know what is. Yes, you heard that correctly, we are fully capable of extreme hate in absolute peace. It's a must try! It's so easy - you just have to have the talk. You may yell, but you may not strike. But, you must emerge at being in complete peace with yourself. I urge the readers to venture on this journey, while being at complete peace with themselves.

As I was writing this book, a strong sense of Kartavyam was driving me to weave the words together in telling you a story. The story of Rama, son of a Chartered Accountant. The man who is fascinated by the world around him. The fictional story tries to capture the complex pathways of the mind of Rama. Although the book has its own stories on Kartavyam, the title is the perfect depiction and an accurate representation of the undercurrent that brought this work into the World.

CHAPTER 1

DISTRACTIONS ABOUND, FOCUS

The boy's name is Vishwath Abhirama, son of a Chartered Accountant. He goes by Rama.

One unsuspecting evening after returning from a full day of work being a sheep, came a book suggestion. Until that moment, Rama wasn't particularly religious or even generally devout. The avid reader he wasn't, downloaded the audio book and started listening to it on his phone.

A self-proclaimed know-it-all, who was an agnostic, turned to this book as his new found religion and became obsessed with the story of what it is to pursue one's destiny. Not unlike the main character of that book, he too was on his way to pursue his own destiny. At barely 23 years old, it seemed like all other doors of pursuit were shut, except for the path he was thrust on to. Which as he recalled, was quite odd. At such a tender age there was only one path for him to walk on. What kind of a crass and uncivilised society forces folks into a path that they can't walk away from?

As is typical of contemporary times, most people are binge watching video content on streaming platforms. The latest trend of spending all the available time on watching videos, shorts, series, and movies is by far the biggest distraction ever created by humanity. One such movie that Rama watched was called Bhaktha Prahlada. A very long time ago there lived a Demon King named Hiranyakashyap who had a son named Prahlada who worshipped his father's nemesis, God Vishnu. This was a matter that caused quite a stir with the Demon King. Hiranyakashyap wants to destroy God Vishnu, who killed his brother. For this purpose he performs an extremely long and difficult tapasya to summon the God Brahma for powers o destroy Vishnu. Brahma could not grant this power as God Vishnu is the preserver and sustainer of Life and asked Hiranyakashyap to make another wish. Then, Hiranyakashyap asked that he may not be killed by any God, Man or an Animal. Brahma grants him the wish, using which he goes on to conquer the three worlds.

Hiranyakashyap in his ungodly way of life of harming the subjects of all 3 worlds, ends up ordering the killing of his own son for the act of worshipping Hari', one of thousand names for God Vishnu. After several failed attempts at killing his own son, he decides to face off with God Vishnu himself and asks his son to show him his beloved Hari. To which Prahalada responds that he may have no doubt as to whether Hari is here or there or is in this or that, because Hari is in everything and everywhere. Agitated King shows his son a pillar and asks if Hari was in this pillar and starts breaking the pillar.

God Vishnu manifests himself, from within the pillar in a half man half lion Avatar, as God Narasimha and tears opens the King in half, saves his young disciple Prahalada and also frees the three worlds from the terror of Hiranyakashyap. This story is as old as time itself and symbolises the victory of good over evil. God Narasimha Avatar is a part of the Ten Avatars of God Vishnu, which also conveys the story of human evolution from Fish to Tortoise to Pig to Narasimha onto more evolved Human Avatars of Vaman, Parashurama, Rama, Krishna, Balaram and Kalki.

The Kalki Avatar, the last of God Vishnu's Dasavatharams is yet to come, and is written to occur at the end of Kali Yuga. After which the Satya Yuga starts again, the first in four of the Chatur Yuga or the Maha Yuga cycle consisting of Satya Yuga, Treta Yuga, Dvapara Yuga and Kali Yuga.

Although the story of Prahlada ends happily, it is filled with pain and suffering. Such a story is typical of the way of life on this planet. There are challenges that need to be overcome to arrive at a preferred state in one's life. World history is filled with such stories. Rarely do we hear another point of view when it comes to people's individual stories and so is also Rama's story.

As we become more and more mature, it becomes ever more difficult to get excited about life or the occurrences in it. Things tend to get insipid overtime and it becomes harder to maintain a sense of enthusiasm about various angles of life. But, there are people that don't show any lack of enthusiasm, they are excited about life. Rama feels jealous about such people and also knows that it's bad to feel jealous about a good thing. With the sheer volume of moving picture content to consume but nothing helpful, Rama decided to lean on black words on white papers to increase the signal ratio in the noise that is persistently bombarding the mind with distractions.

CHAPTER 2

RENTED BODY

The recurring concept of Rent

One day Rama was explaining the concept of Rented body to his wife.

A man has purchased an expensive trash can for the kitchen. It cost him 3000 Rupees. One day his friend visits his home, sees the trash can and asks - "oh, so you rented this one. How much is it per day?".
The man responded - "What rent?! I own it". His friend says, "well, you own it, sure, till it no longer works… then it's thrown away. So, when it's no longer working and you need another to replace it, the ownership status doesn't matter".

The man became curious and asked his friend to continue.

"Let's say you used the trash can for 1000 days (3 years - it's unlikely - but let's assume 1000 for simplicity sake). The rent per day is 3000 divided by 1000 which equals 3 Rupees per day. There you go! You are renting this Trash Can for 3 Rs per day. I introduce you, the concept of rent".

The man was fascinated to see this angle in his ownership of things. He thanked his friend for sharing it with him. As it turned out, the expensive trash can had stopped working after 8 months, and the rent per day for it was calculated to be about 12.5 rupees per day.

Rama continued elaborating on the concept. Our Life, all aspects of it, must be treated as if we (the soul, the spirit) are renting them. This renting also applies to our Body. It applies because, the body also ceases to work one day and you pay the price of Cost of living to use it.

He goes on to expand on the concept by applying the financial principles to this concept of renting one's own body and thereafter to Life itself.

First step in this process would be to take cognisance of the act of Renting. Which means that we chose this Body & Life that came with it. We agreed to the price it took. And, that we did this act in order to achieve some bigger need (a need that transcends lifetimes) that we have. In some unknown or incomprehensible form, we have already paid the down payment or the advance for this body and the life that came with it. Perhaps even signed a contract to account for any moral inconsistencies.

Ability to pay and thus far accumulated credit worthiness, etc., must have also played a role in successfully attaining the lease on the Body and the Life that came with it.

Let's say somebody owns an Expensive car - it's typically safe to assume that that person is an accomplished person. The exceptions would have to be mentioned here, i.e., if someone who has learned the ways of life is faking it to look accomplished - goes out and rents an expensive car for an hour or day - for some purpose. It's wise to be cautious and not be carried away by fakers.

The possibility of Group deals in body rentals can't be ruled out. A group of people with similar needs and interests may be inclined to get together and rent collectively in order to find a more suitable Life and of course gain the pricing advantage along with other well understood compromises.

An example of group renting would be a Family, a collectively Rented entity, where lessees are the family members. A group of souls, before starting on their reunification journey, based on their Karmic Account balance may decide to go with a package rental for their Time on Earth.

Rama's wife had stopped listening a while ago, but that didn't stop him.

By applying this principle back to practical issues of a current life - a family feud would be like a partners in the firm feuding among each other, and this feuding is part of the articles of association, a.k.a, part of the Game. They agreed to play, not so they may always agree but because in the Game laid the Truth. If a standing agreement insisted on always agreeing with each other as the part of playing the game, why play, why not instead simply agree to not play. To voluntarily agree with everything is not the truth that is sought, it is a lazy path to un-enlightenment.

Families and groups, rent the bodies for their Life journeys so they have some help along the way. The Challenge of Life, as is evident to all, is not the easiest and there are times when folks could use some help. Similar to a travel package where if you book as a part of a group all the members get a relief in either the price or gain some other benefits.

This process of renting continues life after life until renting is no longer required. And for some reason unknown to Rama, the memory of the previous life is not easily accessible. Culture reminds that all beings taking new life are a form of reincarnation. The sheer volume of information that needs to be processed in each current life precludes any attempts to try and remember the purpose of renting this life. What is even worse, is to forget that this body and the life that came with it are merely being rented for a purpose that got lost along the way.

Like how a Human Yuga is only one day of Brahma, there may be examples such as of ants, mosquitoes or house flies whose life spans are only a few human days but for those creatures it would be equivalent to a lifetime. Too many lives and too many memories to remember. Which may be why having access to memories of past lives may not be relevant.

A practical application of renting in Real Life is when we buy cheap phones that need replacing every 1-2 years. Or a reasonably priced one that runs greatly for more than 5 years. This decision would determine the rent per day to be higher or lower for having the facility of phone. There is no shame in seeking a lower rent. It means that you want to achieve Moksha in the lowest time possible. Make no mistake - the only payment that is accepted is Time, because time is all you have to give. If you have expensive tastes resulting in a lot of time that's wasted, it might mean that it can take you a while.

Rama looks at his wife, ignoring that she hasn't heard a word, said - "each choice we make on a daily basis determines the rent per day of having that facility in our lives. Keep in mind that this rent is additional to the base rent of the Body & Life Rent that we already pay". She rolls her eyes as they both share a moment of smiles.

CHAPTER 3

Material & Spiritual

Cannot be Separated

Matter and Spirit can't exist in this world without each other. A body without the soul becomes a corpse. Matter usually gets a bad rap because its familiarity bred contempt toward it, while Spirit remained elusive. Balancing one with the other is the challenge of Life. Matter and Spirit are the two sides of the same coin called Life. Abusing one for the sake of another is a commonplace phenomenon and a gross misunderstanding of the ethos of Life.

Of the 2 schools of thought, the School of Matter has largely taken over the mainstream while the School of Spirit has become retreated, limited & restricted to the Esoteric types. Lucky for us, it's not so plain and simple. Just like the Electric & Magnetic field exist together, the spirit of life rises up with every particle of matter.

Let's take an example of you connecting with a person. You could say that connection is either material or spiritual or that it is both. However complex it might seem, it's essential that we go through a reasonable effort to understand whether a connection is spiritual or material. If a person seeks out another person in Friendship and does so for physical backing or support as opposed to an emotional bonding then it would be a material connection, not a spiritual one. The fact the spiritual aspect is lacking creates a chasm that prevents a true connection.

A material example would be a Vehicle that someone buys. They are materially attached to the thing, but when there isn't a sentimental value associated with that vehicle, it merely becomes a tradable object that can be replaced and will most certainly be replaced at the right price. In this case the lack of sentimental value is the lack of a spiritual connection.

The Great Chanakya has said there is no such thing as Friendship with no expectations because friendships occur only when there is some business association, a win-win arrangement for both parties.

It is a harsh thing to say, that there is no such thing as Friendship with no expectations. Children might not take kindly to this rather harsh truth. This single concept could be expanded into consuming an entire book and in many sublime ways, it already is. Precisely put, if there is only one aspect, Matter or Spirit being present in an association, it must be considered an imminent threat that the need for the other will strike back for a balance with vengeance.

Rama had a friend named Prashanth, whom he hadn't initially sought as a friend, with the limited understanding of the concept of friendship at the tender age. Prashanth had one day expressed his friendship toward Rama, who was happy to hear it, and had thenceforth been an unrelenting friend to him. But, Prashanth had moved on to other distractions that were more important. Rama was disappointed and learned after a long spell of non-reciprocated friendship that it was his own naivety that had allowed this suffering.

The same thing happened with others in other contextual interactions, where Rama himself wasn't desirous of a connection but the others' initiative had impressed upon him an obligation to be truly true to the connection. Later on it turns out that Rama was the only one committed, while the others had no intentions of reciprocation or had long moved away from their commitments.

This was because, Rama was only offering the Spiritual contribution on his part without fully comprehending the complex ways of life and that there was also the need to ensure that the material needs be offered for the connection to sustain. This was a very hard pill to swallow as by the time this truth was realised, Rama had lost almost all of his connections. If it wasn't for the concept of the Rented body and its principle of continuing lives with accrued balance of good deeds, our beloved Rama would have become quite a spectacle.

Rama said to himself, "there was no need to be upset about all the things I have lost nor there is reason to be excited for the future good that may come from this new discovery of the concept of inability of Nature to separate the Spirit from its Matter and the opposite". And went on to explain to himself that, "this is the work, the suffering is the work - it isn't the money that you made from your work on the planet, but the suffering you have endured in this journey of working on yourself. Not to mention that knowing the concept is only part of it, applying it is an entirely different beast to tame".

After long hours of thinking, he was able to attribute the root cause of almost all the suffering in this world to be traced back to the individual's inability to comprehend this basic truth, that they may not allow for the separation of the spiritual and material beings and that they both complement and complete each other.

Rama goes on an introspective conversation with himself to explore the depths of his latest discovery.

'What exactly is the point of this concept? Like any knowledge, it's about becoming wiser through its application. As a Walker is a tool for the kids to learn walking, this concept would become a tool that one can use for self discovery. A real life use case would go something similar to these lines... In the Life cycle, where you as the Head of the Family are leading a family of three generations, with two or more generations on both sides of your timeline, i.e., Children - the next generation and the Parents - the previous generation.

As your children are increasing in their physical and cognitive abilities, your parents are losing these abilities. The kids are going in one direction while the elders are going in the opposite direction. Inevitably, you will be exhausted from scrambling between them. With respect to this particular physical and cognitive capabilities, the task is to enable the kids to increase the push forward and for the elders to push back the changes in their physical and cognitive abilities and to keep them healthy and fit as much as possible. Some might immediately respond by saying, they both need nutritious and balanced diets. They are not wrong but also are not fully right.

Healthy diet will help physical well being and also cognitive well being to a certain extent. This is where we apply the Inseparability of Material and Spiritual Worlds. We assume that in providing food ends the responsibility and we have removed all commotion and restored harmony to the household, problem solved and we move on. However, if the commotion still persists, it's imperative to assess by putting the food in the Material column and start thinking about what will balance it in the Spiritual column. One way could be where you personally are present at the time of eating with your Children and Parents - spend quality time, and in more than just words letting them know that you are always there for them no matter what. See if that helps!

The needs of these generations may differ from time to time and from topic to topic. When these needs are not met it can create commotion in the household, which within itself has the innate ability to spiral out of control. This is exactly where this concept can become your tool or weapon of choice to diffuse the commotion and take back control of your family.

The process is pretty straight forward. Identify what you are providing whether it is spiritual or material or if it's varying combinations of both, and then work toward achieving the balance between them.

As this concept can come handy to folks - it's worth taking another shot at it to explain further the various angles and depths this might mean.

Family was the previous example. Another example is of Friendship. In this illustration we take a look at the social construct we typically address as Friendship.
Let's start with the basic premise that after Family, Friendship is by far the most meaningful experience one might experience in their lifetimes. Which is why it is that much more difficult to take an axe to it, but it must be done lest ignore the problems in Friendship and forever regret not addressing those ahead of time.

Rama is in agreement with The Great Chanakya that there is no such thing as Friendship without expectations. It's not easy to type these words as there are way too many folks who have built their entire lives on the concept of Friendship. It is by no means intended to hurt their sentiments, in fact sentiments are those that add meaning and value to things. But, what's known to you must be said, so folks can make up their own minds.

When something that was never defined or taught, and general proximity determines who qualifies as friends - on the face of it, it sounds pretty childish - because by the same definition when people move away or drift apart, they would no longer qualify to be friends. This is precisely what happens to a lot of Friendships. Such a superficial concept, with almost no depth, cannot possibly be taken seriously as a contender in being one of the most amazing experiences of Life.

Each has their definitions and to what extent they are willing to go or do for the well being of their friends. In a contest to one-up each other, or just to show off their "virtues" to others - folks end up using their friends to further personal agendas. It all seems pretty harmless until you start taking stock about the price being paid and by whom. It's not a fair world and for reasons not so obvious, the way the world works is perhaps elusive for a reason more important than it is important for all to understand it.

In limiting this exploration to this particular flavour of shallow friendships, it is worth noting that friendships are built on Trust; and for some reason the trust setting is set to a default of Trusting everybody, except in the circumstances that are affecting everyone. In such a setting - the truly virtuous and the unfortunate innocents are the ones from whom most toll is exacted. They pay the highest price of admission and they end up paying the highest toll regardless of the distance they travel on this road called Friendship.

This abusive setup is possible because of the lack of understanding of the concept of inseparability of the spiritual and material worlds. Once we apply this concept to friendships - friendships suddenly become more stronger because a balanced approach gets activated. Where friends are not just about partying (material needs) with each other but also about participating in each other's lives in a deeper sense where you enquire about each other's spiritual well being and ensure your friends are doing okay.

Friendships where such an approach cannot be activated - they are bound to leave an unpleasant aftertaste for all parties involved, some more than others. As Rama is going deeper and deeper into his mind - he can sense that he is venturing into dangerous territories.

A real world relatable illustration of the toll you pay, owing to the virtue of your individual existence and your circumstances, is when your Dentist peeks out of the window to check the size of your car to decide how much you will pay for the services or treatment he provides you. The bigger the car, the higher you pay.

This way of doing business will seem unfair to those who are being charged more and for those who are being charged less, it'll seem quite fair, in a very limited view of things rather than a generalised view. Although Rama has an opinion on this matter, he is normally not in a position to challenge the status quo, therefore will have to suffer the consequences and may sometimes enjoy the advantages.

Such is the deep entanglement of matter and spirit in our daily lives. Comprehending them both is in itself a herculean task, even more so mastering it.

Rama goes on to question the similar nature of the Concept of Love with the concept of friendship and swiftly arrives at the same conclusion that the concept of Love is so misunderstood, even more so, misapplied and misused. Combining the Inseparability of Material and Spiritual Worlds (IMSW) with Love may also come quite handy for some.

The IMSW concept has so much to offer so why not use this opportunity to explore one last topic on it to expand a bit more before moving onto the next thought on his mind, thought Rama.

Just because something is achieved using money doesn't mean it falls in the category of Material. For example, take the school fee for children, where the parent spends all his budget on the fee for an expensive school with no other involvement from the Parents, it would definitely fall in the material column with very little spirit to the act.

But, if the parent chooses to go for a reasonable and optimally priced school by spending about half his budget and using the other half he spends on other activities such as recreation, visiting parks and buying educational toys which help in overall and a better learning. All this in combination with an active participation of the parents in their child's development, would fall into a balanced spiritual and material contribution.

An unfortunate reality is that almost all available material and spirit have become so intricately intertwined with money. As a result, one's ability to provide material support along with the spiritual support has become unquestionably restricted. Whoever controls money, effectively, controls all life. Material does not exercise any control in this situation but Spirit on the other hand will choose to be crushed before it'll allow itself to be centrally controlled. Which is probably why there are relentless campaigns underway to manipulate and corrupt the spirit.

Whoever chooses to control all money - thereby exercising control and restricting people's material support to each other, has the mental capacity of a scattered brain and hence can never understand the role of the spirit in bringing things truly together.

CHAPTER 4

WHAT IS BUSINESS?

Explanation of Way of Life

Rama was always fascinated with business because it is what drives people. In his mind business should not be something that exploits people off their life savings. It's what explains the way of life to people so they may save themselves. When a fruit seller is going from street to street pushing his cart, he isn't just relying on the good graces of his customers to earn a living, he is sure that his customers are naturally wired to want the nutrients from the fruits he's holding.

He also has a few tools up his sleeve that tell him that if he dials down the price a bit, he can sell off all of his fruits and head home quicker and when he doesn't have a lot going on, he can jack up the price and make the most money. The other angle is that the customer knows the seller needs the money he holds to meet his non-fruit needs and he too can use the tools he has to get the most fruit for the least money by bargaining a bit or buying in bulk, etc., you get the point. This is business and a small example of a way of life.

A student who is enrolled in a school learns what is taught in the classroom. The younger the mind the harder the message hits. A college graduate who was taught everything he knows in the classroom may not have a clue what it takes to conquer the smallest challenge he faces outside of his protected bubble environment.

On the other hand, a street smart child who has learned a substantial portion of his skills from his business-running parents understands and sees the world way more clearly than his counterparts on the other side. Does this knowledge ever spillover to other students with non-business-running parents? Even though the probability exists, its practical possibility is non-existent. One reason for this is that the Business secrets are closely guarded as it means life and death of that business. Another reason is that the uncertainty of the Business ecosystem in the Indian Markets for several decades has completely shunned off all middle income families from ever looking to pursue a business.

Typical middle class parents never encourage their children to pursue business. A middle class Indian must work as an employee of a business and must never dream of running such a business, is the mindset. Sure, you know a friend who has overcome all odds and become a successful businessman. Unfortunately, that person is an exception and not the rule and that is the problem. It shouldn't be an exception to run a business. It should be the rule.

Business is how Life chooses to conduct itself. In business we see what the needs are, what it takes to meet those needs, why these need to be met, what happens if they aren't, where is the supply, where is the demand and how things can be made better? If one thinks these things can be taught in a classroom, their teachers failed them.

Business is how people become interdependent while still maintaining an extremely free way of life and preserving their right to choose. An example is that we all are dependent on Milk in order to provide a healthy diet to our families, ergo interdependent on the farmer or the dairy cooperative society to provide the milk we need. But, should it be realised that the Milk producer is cutting corners and providing a lower quality or harmful milk, the customer retains the right to go to another Milk provider. This is Business, it's very personal as it means the well being of the family.

In the absence of this atmosphere of teaching checks and balances and a needed attitude of innate responsibility to its children, their curious minds wander off chasing the shiniest objects they see. Children want to be Airforce Pilots, Musicians, Singers, Actors, Politicians, CMs, PMs, without the faintest idea, why?

Even though it is no one's business what someone wants to become, it becomes everyone's business when that someone chooses to be responsible for a task that affects everyone.

The reason why someone wants to become an Actor is very very less important than why an Actor wants to become a CM or a PM. This is Business, the very personal business where an acclaimed actor for his amazing skills of performance arts earned the following of Millions of Fans. But, it becomes very much a Business matter of public interest when hidden sources of funding are backing an actor into becoming a Leader of peoples.

Another aspect that is endorsed in Business is that Businesses build wealth. Wealth earned by good people in honest ways is a definite good. This wealth ends up strengthening the families enough to support many more other families, in the form of opportunities derived, short-term and long-term employment created, knowledge and skill development possibilities, etc.

Rama has failed at Business so many times it has become a running joke in his own mind whenever he comes up with a new business idea. Little did he know, at the time of investing in his ideas, that he had no idea how or why a business succeeds. A good idea, it seems, is a sure shot way to waste your life savings in pursuing it as a business. Rama has stopped all his business pursuits, for the time being, as it came as no surprise to him that he had no business doing business he doesn't fully understand.

A communist or socialist or capitalist book would drive the minds to the injustices and inequities of the system that it opposes. Yet somehow the efforts to create the new utopia, invariably result in creating a much worse off version than its predecessor.

Rama's mind was also drawn towards the wealth of the society. How wealth is created and becomes acquired? What gives the wealthy their legitimacy?

There is a very auspicious ceremony that happens in a Bharathiya Household. It is the SatyaNarayana Vratam Puja. It is believed that whoever performs or even listens to this puja with devotion and concentration will have their wishes fulfilled. It's an amazingly powerful ritual. In one of the stories recited during this puja and many other pujas as is customary of Households, the birth of a child into a wealthy household comes as a result of his or her previous life's good deeds. This is quite a convenient narrative to prevent any punitive action against the wealthy - which is why Rama doesn't subscribe to it. One may be very wealthy but doesn't have a moment to spend with his family is the perfect example of a pauper.

Wealth is not a bad thing in our society. Wealth was never a bad thing in our society. Wealthy people have taken it to be their duty to uplift the society that may not be so fortunate. But, there must be public oversight into accumulation of wealth, the means of acquisition and its utilisation.

It has come to be accepted that the Child of the Parent deserves the wealth earned by the Parent because it's Natural Law to bequeath the result of the hard work of a parent be useful for the needs of their offspring, assuming that those earnings were honest.

But, when the earnings are ill-gotten and through dishonest means, the passing on of said wealth shall not be allowed. Because, if it were to happen, that becomes the slippery slope Humanity can never climb up from. The moral hazard is simply too dangerous to ignore.

In the immature years Rama recalls his attempts to share with his mother his understanding of the world, owing to which his perspective and what he wants to do with his life has changed. But, his simple mother who caused the changes didn't approve of his attitude or the actions he has taken to further his agenda. In his own small way, this was Rama's attempt to understand the Business that was his Life and thereby realising his purpose in it.

Rama quickly realised the connection between Concept of Business - about explaining the way of life to people so they may save themselves and how this is also related to the Construct of Friendship. The material and spiritual needs have to be met for both. Additionally, a certain way to ensure a long standing friendship is to have some sort of a business relationship.

When we were trying for meaningful friendships in our meaningless lives - it wasn't working - genuine efforts were nevertheless rendering only hollow friendships. One may quickly realise that there are no real friends and no such thing as true friendship - there are only partners with mutually beneficial understandings. The sooner one realises this the better their "friendships" will become.

Of all the experiences Rama had in his Life, barring a few exceptions, it had become clear that almost every connection was commercially or other agenda driven. With every new experience he was becoming an improved man. He now realises that just because a connection wanted your help doesn't mean they had nothing good they brought to you, it just means they need some help and if you are in a position to help, help, else try to maintain the connection until such time help can be offered, because that is Life.

All those affected by the business of love may take this under advisement. Instead of saying "I love you", say, "you're my Life" and then everything will start to make sense. There is no Love or Friendship or other imaginary constructs, there is only Life. All other dreamed up concepts simply confuse us away from the true understanding of Life. Family is the closest we ever came to Life and when harm comes anywhere near Family, it's Family Business. When a Business runs like a Family and harm comes to it, it becomes everyone's business. Rama thought to himself, "Family is Business and Business is Family". He made a mental note that he must remember this every time he handles a family matter or conducts business.

Rama was starting to see the light. His Life and its place in the world was slowly starting to make sense. He was sure that there must have been so many of his predecessors who saw these Truths. How come he is stuck realising these the hard way? There must surely be hundreds of books that captured these Truths. The best example Rama can recall was , "It's not personal, it's strictly business" and it too sends the wrong message.

There are so many harsh truths to learn in the store, yet, here we are where billions of people are stuck laughing at a never ending stream of caricature and slapstick stuff that are passed off as comedy and entertainment. "Wake up Rama", he told himself!

CHAPTER 5
TO CONQUER

the Truth

Thus far Rama has realised that there can be way too many distractions placed in the way of an Individual with the specific intent to make him sway away from his destiny.

He explored the role of the body one wears. The Material and Spiritual needs and how they have to be balanced and his latest quotable quote about "Family is Business and Business is Family".

As the unease is keeping Rama close to the edge, he continues to want to push the blame on to someone other than himself for the lack of enlightenment and the other obvious facts of his non-existent accomplishments. But, if he's going to earn a bare minimum of brownie points, Rama would have to prove his worth. Blaming someone solves nothing. It may potentially result in a cluster feud with people pointing fingers in every direction including the time dimension.

Even still, to assess a person or diagnose a problem, it's generally considered a good starting point to look at the surroundings, the circumstances and then digging at what exists, what changed, etc.

Typically what changed for Rama wasn't of much help, because not much has changed in his life and on the other hand, he doesn't really know what changed in the lives of those who are affecting him. There is a saying, Yadhartha vaadhi loka virodhi - which translates as, the one who speaks the Truth is the enemy of the people. Rama understood that this couldn't possibly be true. Just like another popular saying Ahimsa Paramo Dharma Ha, which as it turns out is incomplete and therefore misleading and when uttered incompletely is utter nonsense.

Inspired by the discovery about the utter nonsensical usage of Ahimsa Paramo Dharma Ha, Rama came up with a complete version which explains why it is that speaking the truth is not enough. When speaking the truth, the speaker must himself first learn the way to achieve it, then achieve it and only then speak it unto others, so they may also achieve it for themselves.

It is important to show how the Truth can be achieved, otherwise what good does learning a truth do when it's unattainable. And those who cannot show the path but simply utter the Truth's are, deservedly so, treated as enemies of people.

Speaking the Truth, although it sounds like it's the Right thing to do, it doesn't matter. Just because someone told you that something is True doesn't make it true. Your work of successfully verifying its veracity is what makes it True. Your work in overcoming this Truth to bring about the needed change that you so desire, is the work of conquering the Truth. The real work of conquering the Truth, is the Journey that unlocks the person's potential of his Life's work. After all, isn't conquering the Truth the most worthy of life goals ?!

To conquer the Truth isn't a one time activity but a lifestyle. When the endless stream of knowledge noise comes bombarding you through all the channels available, the sheer volume can be overwhelming. The act of conquering the Truth from so much noise can be like finding a needle in a haystack. Simply put, that is a job not best suited for the faint hearted.

Therefore the task of handling a common truth may be delegated with utmost care.

Truth isn't about spewing venom using the facts. Truth as much as one would like to generalise it, isn't general at all. Truth is Personal. Your Journey with the Truth helps you alone, as much as you may think you are doing all of this for others. That's just something that may help you measure the progress you are making, but it always has and will be about you.

The Person's need for Truth is existential in its Nature. This must be understood well for becoming self aware. Otherwise, we end up becoming clueless wanderers in the vastness of nothingness. It mustn't be the death bed where people realise that they have lived complete meaningless lives. It must be done so, as early and as far away from the end as possible. The sooner this is realised the more progress one can achieve in their conquest of Truth within this lifetime.

Rama realised that the lack of this understanding about the Truth is what caused the immeasurable suffering that his country endured over several centuries. Somewhere along the line the Gurus dropped the ball on teaching the lessons about Truth, and when faced with danger, the society fell like a pack of cards. Indians had always thought that they were doing the Right thing when they naively welcomed the veiled invaders with an attitude of Athidi Devo Bhava (Guest is God). If you were an invader who is treated like God, won't you be tempted to take advantage of the naivety of your host. Anyone would!

This is not to argue that Indians must stop doing the Right thing. We mustn't leave our virtue, we must continue. However, the attitude of doing the right thing must always be done so in conjunction with one's journey of conquering the Truth. Rama thought to himself, let's apply this right now and see if Doing the Right Thing on our Conquest of Truth could have potentially prevented the centuries long suffering of Indians.

On the journey to conquer the Truth, you would have been forced to reckon as to why a guest would have come to you. Before extending a free reign over all that is yours, you would subject them to the same level of scrutiny as you would do to yourself when you may be visiting a foreign country.

The low hanging fruits usually would be something like the need for money or food and you are so desperate that you are knocking on doors. Let's assume that being desperate for food is indeed the fact of why your guest has come knocking. Fact does not equal Truth. Truth is when the facts are translated and their after effects are properly assessed. A hungry neighbour, who learns about your abundance of food and your attitude of generosity, will attempt to take unfair advantage of you. This impending potential of conflict and resulting suffering must be overcome successfully, while still being true to doing the right thing. Feeding your guest, treating him like god and doing nothing more, because God would never take unfair advantage of you - would be equal to you conquering this particular Truth.

Rama thought that this kind of thinking should have been taught to him in school. Learning about something that is so personal in the context of something so general, and also testing the waters of the opposite way, could have been such a fun-filled learning activity to do in school. Having such knowledge could help avoid many embarrassments.

Chapter 6
Don't Fuss

Think ahead

Thinking of all the past embarrassments, Rama was a bit disappointed at the help and guidance he had received in his younger years. Although he is not one to point fingers or blame others he only keeps remembering things so he may not repeat the same mistakes. Without a doubt, it is the best course of action to not fuss about the past but instead to think ahead.

As the boy's journey would have it, he was guided in many ways to not take the job he was offered but instead be flown off to distant lands in search of the unachievable happiness-in-a-box.

Even though the modern transportation made Rama feel like the distant lands were indeed only a night flight away from home, the distance in reality was truly close to Infinity. When the astounding numbers of those returning home from said distant lands was astonishingly close to zero, the real distance on the return ticket home is unreachable.

This is not just because they don't let you go, the society has become so brainwashed that your own family won't let you come back. Rama knew upon his first failed attempt to return, that this uphill battle was going to cost him dearly.

The monopolising of the marketplace happened not through physical violence, but through mental subjugation of the masses. It was a battle for the brains, where India suffered the brain drain, while those with much higher currency conversion rates benefited tremendously from the abundance of cheap labour that this currency situation created.

Indian leaders surely knew about this terrible fate that was being imposed on lakhs of unsuspecting youths, but also couldn't stop the aspirational young minds, by painting a big-picture doomsday scenario. Largely speaking, it is yet to be fully comprehended by those leaving the country, about the real price being paid in terms of non-money units. The loss of the family unit is just one of the many. The disconnect from the culture and society. The effects of inadvertently becoming an outsider and then becoming stuck in that limbo for a long time. The confused offspring and an overall distortion is the real price.

Rama, since the day he landed in the distant land, was desperate to return. He realised his mistake. It took its toll but eventually Rama returned. Since then he has become an advocate, not just to himself, but to each and everyone. The logic according to him was very simple. If you can't succeed at your home base, your supposed success at a foreign base cannot be treated as legitimate, mainly because it's not transferable.

Transfer here is not about the transfer of money but is about the transfer of the person. When the person and his family can't return, his success will not be allowed to come home. Ultimately, it's the person who can succeed and not his money. It's only when the person along with all of his family truly returns home, only then can his success be considered to be transferred back along with him.

Rama had no idea at the time of leaving why he was leaving the Country, except for the fact that he was being herded along with many of his countrymen. Not only was he being removed from his ancestral homeland, but also being saddled with a debt burden which would be insurmountable without toiling away in the distant land for a long period of time. Any one who has left the country without the feeling of a financial burden is bound to swiftly return. You can take the man out of poverty but you can't take the poverty out of his mind, thought Rama.

The world wasn't being run in the quest of knowledge but driven by the lack there of it. It's like insider trading, only a few know what's really happening and only they will benefit the most.

His core belief of doing the right thing and treating guests like gods, was in question. When you are an unwelcome guest in a distant land, who is perceived as being there to steal their jobs you can't be a guest. As an immigrant with an intention to make a life there, your treatment is bound to be a response proportional to your intentions.

There can never be an open discussion between the immigrants and the locals because it would immediately be tagged as being discriminatory. The locals never really understand the newcomers and the immigrants stay in a state of mistrust. An individual with his best efforts may barely scratch the surface of the playing field of race relations repair.

Not to pile on, but the chasm between people who through no fault of their own are categorised forever into impenetrable silos, have to break those walls in order to see the Truth. The most superficial of ways to look at this situation is that you've identified a behaviour that will surely bother you again someday. Simply recognise that it's not a flaw, but a feature that is going to work in your favour one day. Be thankful you have the blessing of witnessing your future ammunition in advance.

CHAPTER 7
HEART BEAT

Goes With the Flow, with Zero Guidance

The music that makes up our life as it goes on playing. The heart beat is programmed to try and synchronise with other hearts around it so there can be harmony among humans. But this understanding would be for the simpleton, who hasn't yet arrived at the realisation that the world didn't start with his birth and won't end with his death.

The heart wants harmony. The "smart" ones in the past have long figured out what the Human Heart has been programmed to behave like, and have since started using this knowledge against it.

The Heart is being pushed into a trap from which it can't escape. The beat it's playing is trapping the mind from thinking anything else but to remain in this trap. It's evident that the heart will follow his fellow humans all the way into the abyss in an entrapment misleadingly named Harmony.

Yet another intriguing aspect of the Heartbeat is its importance in identifying, differentiating and confirming reality. But, this is not being used. What is one supposed to do when a high performance mind can imagine things so vividly, that from a documented memory in the brain, it is impossible to say which is Reality and which and imagination?

The brain is actively engaged in imagining various possibilities and scenarios that it deems necessary at the time. The brain, to its credit, is also running its reality on an auto pilot mode quite efficiently. The obvious downside to this auto-pilot and an overactive imagination is that the reality will not be documented in close detail. The imagination, on the other hand, with all its vivaciousness, becomes burned in memory forever.

Which is probably why Rama, who has just started observing his heartbeat closely, is slowly realising the reason why he can't remember much of his day to day routine activities. Only vague recollections and obscure details may be recovered.

One sunny afternoon on a winter day, Rama went on a trip with some friends. They took a boat to the middle of the sea to see the coral reefs. After jumping into the sea, Rama with the help of snorkelling gear was hanging on to a rope and viewing all the bright colours in the form of fish. The sheer volume of fish was an instant sight of happiness. There was so much colourful life he hadn't even imagined until that moment. This image is perhaps what they call a life changing event, he thought. He felt the presence of God in seeing his creation.

But, this moment of awe didn't last long. As he sensed a tension on the rope he was holding, he came above the surface of the water to find that one of his friends was in a state of panic. Filled with fear he was trying to climb onto the rope, which was strictly instructed as a not to do action, as it can jeopardise the safety of all the people holding the rope.

Others signalled the lifeguard for help, but his friend was unknowingly determined to drown them all, as he was vehemently trying to put his feet on the rope. In this moment, Rama could sense that his end was near but was not bothered by it. He thought that this is how it ends and went back to enjoying the underwater beauty for however little time it might last.

To everyone's relief the lifeguard swam over and pulled Rama's friend away from the rope and helped him onto the boat. Only a few short weeks after this trip an underwater rig exploded in the gulf and basically ruined the entire ecosystem. The moment when he heard this news, how all colourful life spilling over was upended with one oil spill, it felt like a personal tragedy. When he visited a far away beach a few years later and there he could see the tar balls from that oil spill, his heart skipped a beat.

When imagination takes control, keeping in touch with one's heartbeat will help them stay in reality. Your Heartbeat as your witness what you experience is your reality. He thought, I must occasionally physically feel it with my palm so as to not lose touch.

Rama kept on pondering...

We all know that the heart beats, and we think that is why we are living. In thinking and doing so we are proving the negative and thereby assuming the opposite is true - because we die when the heart stops beating, we are settling for - heart beats keeps us alive.

What about the other possibility? Could it be that the heart beat is an effect and not the cause. Rama thinks that because he is living, therefore his heart beats. But, why else could the heart keep beating? Rama thinks that the heart beats to keep the frequencies of spirit and the matter synced together, so one doesn't escape the other.

Like a piece of code in the DNA written somewhere inside that that's what this spirit and matter combination was put together to do, be tied together, for some purpose. And, when there is no more hope left for the spirit or when it has achieved all it possibly can, it tells the heart to take rest. Heart doesn't stop beating, just like the lungs don't stop breathing by their own volition, it's ordered to do so, most likely by the spirit himself.

CHAPTER 8

BANKRUPTCY

Moral bankruptcy occurs before the Fiscal

When someone is fiscally bankrupt, one would be ill advised to vouch for their timely debt paying virtues. It's a harsh and heartless statement to make and there are exceptions to it. Exceptions to this rule are Bad luck, fraud and/or disadvantages from birth circumstances.

From all the good values we try to teach the kids with the best of intentions, they grow up and see the real world for what it is and become disillusioned by it.

Rama has seen a movie, which was quite successful for many reasons. The construct where the perceived reality is simulated to feel like real life ... where in the actual reality the humans are harvested for their body heat as batteries that are used to run the machines. For now, let's just be open to the idea that our planet and life as we can best comprehend it could all very well be a simulation.

Add to that, the most basic tenets of Human coexistence. The basic tenets may be believed to be different for different people, but Rama is of the impression, it is the same for us all. The most basic tenet, according to him, is that Humans don't get along with each other. This is based on the immense potential each human has and therefore other Humans are naturally perceived as potential adversaries and obstacles on their path to Destiny. This phenomenon in its various forms can sometimes manifest itself as hatred.

Even though the underlying reasons for all the seemingly senseless wars, useless drama and meaningless dialogue are self-evident, we are forced to believe the opposite. To be conditioned to see only the good in people can mean deliberate omissions of wrongdoings and granting unwilling forgiveness for crimes committed. To put his manifested hatred aside will certainly take a toll on the man, i.e., addictions, frustrations, violations, etc. In such a setting where even the beloved offspring are not spared from this wrath for long, one can only imagine the lack of mercy shown to strangers.

Rama thought to himself, "I pity those who get stuck in the ideology imbibed into them at an early age and are unable to break out of shackles of Human naivety, mainly because it was the parents who imbibed these values into them. After all, who would think that their own Parents could knowingly set their Children up for failure, pain and misery. The Child upon turning an adult can fathom that his Parents had no clue why they were teaching what they were teaching. Upon turning a parent, hopefully he does not repeat the same mistakes. Or, maybe being lazy and being lousy parents is part of our programming, like a default setting".

All these shortcomings on the part of the person, account for the moral bankruptcy that is bound to take over one's life. Where life itself will tend to become an endless stream of travel from one chore to the next. On this journey, borrowing money and not paying back feels justified because he truly believes that the system has failed him and therefore he has no longer any interest to contribute to such a system.

Rama sympathises with such a person because when society is simply reduced to a bunch of transactions occurring with no meaning, disenchantment with it isn't a deviation but a completely expected outcome.

Let's assume the planet and the life on it were indeed a simulation, where only a very small percentage of people can even understand the real reality of the way things are and a much less percentage of these can even comprehend doing something about it. Then, the simulation idea will start to make sense.

Imagine yourself being a game designer or a puppet master who is simulating and simultaneously producing a live streaming reality television series for experimentation / entertainment / elimination purposes. The parameters we have are perfect. Give each Human a unique ability and fill them full of potential with vast capabilities both physical and mental. Arm them with organisational skills and also fully equip them to fight with physical strength. Add to the mix, billions of people, waking up with the Sun to compete with each other for basic survival. All these and other things present here are what constitute a really large test tube in a grand lab. Like some quality testing facility in a factory, where each piece produced must go through a rigorous testing before it can be passed onto the next phase.

We may only go about this far in our imagination but if we think we can fully understand what this game is about - we would be delusional.

A best effort guess would be, where each one of these billions are being tested for every capability given, for decisions taken and for every action that is done and not done. Just imagining the sheer volume of data that's churning inside this simulator machine would increase our core body temperature.

Which brings us to the ultimate question, why?

Why such a huge production? Certainly not to prove one's virtues to others? Is it to test whether we know what virtues are better? Or is it to test whether we really understand why some virtues are better over others? And what exactly is the point of proving it to others?

This line of questions reminded Rama of the story of the two mice that fell into the bucket of cream, while one drowned the other churned the cream into butter and walked out of the bucket. The only difference here is the numbers. How many of them will drown and how many survive in a similar human survival test ?

There are plenty of well known stories that send useful messages but how many are really being applied. Between knowing and doing, Knowing maybe Life, but Doing is, certainly, More Life. Fiscal bankruptcy is like drowning by not swimming, because we know how to avoid it, but won't do anything to stop it. This happens because our morals were bankrupt, resulting in shackling ourselves to inaction.

Rama thought to himself, "Moral bankruptcy happens before Fiscal".

Rama has no desire to give hope one way or another about potential solutions to problems. Because, there are few solutions that can help from the outside. Solutions only exist outside when the problems exist outside. But, most problems don't exist outside of our physical being.

No matter the number of sermons given, motivations muzzled, movies made, people will continue to manifest a disliking towards each other, certainly not immediately, but as time goes on and their individual interests are in conflict with each other. It's not a flaw, it's a feature. A feature that will enable the bringing forth of a better self, not necessarily unto others but unto themselves.

If there is a glimmer of Hope that is worth a mention, that is the Rule of Law. The only thing preventing people from going bonkers from all this pent up animosity among themselves is the social contract that is enabled by all the various Rules and Laws of the land.

The role of the rule of law can never be overstated. It is granted that the current rules are far from perfect, but this is where we are as a society and the duty to improve these rules is also upon the citizens.

Rama therefore is of the strong belief that Rules and Laws are all we have separating us from Anarchy; the word Anarchy may sound cool but is nothing close to it in actuality. A deliberate mockery of the rules with no respite in the form of correction or improvement, can be easily attributed to work of propagandists conspiring to pull off yet another trick to fool the public.

It should not take a scientist to figure out how hard the powers that be are working to prevent progress in the name of progress, deliver injustice in the name of justice, wreak havoc in the name of governance and most importantly a strict preservation of the status quo in the name of perpetual change, growth and development.

If you think that a popular book named after a calendar year is a dystopia far in the future, think again. It actually has been a permanent present for at least a century. The book wasn't about the future, it was written about the contemporary times of the Author's Life. Although, the reason for naming that book after a future year may have confused a few people for a few years until the year has passed. In the contemporary times of this book, there is no longer any confusion that said dystopia is a fully alive, living and breathing phenomenon.

Rama was lost in thought, scrambling to find a solution or at least a direction to the solution. He thought, the Rule of Law is the only tool there is and these Rules and Laws designed by the People they serve, should in themselves be a self improving mechanism to prevent abuse and preserve themselves.

CHAPTER 9

CIRCLE OF CIRCUMSTANCE

Will Help You Strike the Balance

On his journey, Rama came across several wise souls, who have inspired within him an alter ego of sorts, the wise soul within, who teaches important life lessons. He came up with the concept of Circle of Circumstance that helped clarify a lot of issues. This particular lesson intuitively made sense to him.

There is a very old saying recommending that drinking water without any effort is to be preferred over drinking milk achieved after effort. A similar saying would be that of a Bird in Hand worth Two in a Bush. Being content with what you have, is perhaps in the top 10 life philosophies of all time.

What exactly is Life really about? Is it to chase after whatever is reaching out to you, or is it not to chase after anything but to find solace in whatever and wherever it is you find yourself.

The narrative we choose to subscribe to can help define our attitude toward life, similar to how the circumstances we go through define the way we shape our lives. The Circle of circumstance tells us that the range of the circumstances isn't a linear spectrum that stretches from left to right, but rather a spectrum that goes around in a circle.

An example of one such circle of circumstance can be visualised if we plot the number of friends and the amount of money one has, on a circular graph - the image will show that the Richest and the Poorest are the ones with the least number of Friends, while those in the middle income are the ones with the most friends.

Even such a simple observation is often ignored. The fact that someone who has a bigger circle of friends is incorrectly assumed to be Rich. India's Richest Man doesn't have a big circle of friends, he simply has a lot of business relations and transactions that bring a lot of people to him. If anything, he has a lot of enemies vying and scheming to steal from him.

The point of this exercise isn't to gauge an optimal size of your circle of friends, but to identify the circumstances you are currently in and the circumstances you seek to be in, in the future. This way you can check the number of friends you may, on your preferred path, lose or gain. Another way to look at the same circle, is when we don't have a lot of worldly connections, one can become extremely successful or the exact opposite.

There are several applications of the circle of circumstance. Here is another example to illustrate the concept. Those with the highest responsibility when not careful, are also dangerously close to doing the least responsible thing.

The point of the Circle of circumstance is for us to realise that it's not about blindly following the flow in one direction or the other but, for us to recognise and strike the balance with life, where we can live a life of peace with ourselves. Applying the Circle of circumstance will help you strike the balance.

In applying the circle of circumstance to our most sacred duty, Kartavyam, we realise that Moksha is our Kartavyam. It is important to realise where you are on the Circle and in which direction you have to go to attain Moksha. And also realising that Moksha is attainable in both directions on the circle and that you may take the long route or the short route.

But this is not how the Author of one of the books Rama read, chose to advise the boy, by the way of the wise man. Instead the advice, which was coined a secret, says to enjoy life but not to forget one's duties. It was such a cliche. Very convenient for the Author to say, unfortunately it was an easy-to-say, harder-to-do, kind of advice. It was advised to divide attention between tasks. When focus is divided, that's when important things get missed. When there are two tasks at hand, it's best to team up with others that suit well for the task.

The best example of team work resulting in the most wonderful of experiences on the planet is that of Marriage. The wife wants to live in the moment while the husband wants to have the perfect ending. When they both come together, they get to live in the moment and have a perfect ending.

Moral of the story shouldn't be that focus must be divided. In such a case the expectations are set in a way that no one's ever good enough. The Moral should be that we are all good enough for whatever little we set out to achieve and get done.

The usual casualty of divided attention is the unit of Family. It needs nurturing and care. It takes a lot to run a Family correctly and when family gets a second priority that's when things go awry.

Family is not an all powerful unit. It's a decently strong and somewhat self-sustaining entity, but family is more appropriately defined as a building block that gains strength as more blocks come together in unity, in building a bigger family-like unit, a stronger society.

Because, oftentimes, a family which is constituted by Humans, has full potential to cause serious damage to its constituents and other families around. Owing to competing interests of fully potent individuals, self-sabotage by other family members, non-alignment of worldview, non-meeting of expectations and inherited reparable and irreparable damage done by the predecessors, a family can be a powder keg ready to explode or be in a constant state of war with itself.

Visualise where you are and where your family is on the Circle of circumstance, and then visualise where you want yourself to be and where you want your family to be. After proper assessment, you may act in the interest of your family.

Chapter 10
HELP YOURSELF

To Help is Really Not a Choice

One morning as Rama was attending to his chores on his motorcycle, a youngster about college age accompanied by a primary school boy holding a badminton racquet held out his hand seeking a lift and uttered the name of the school he wanted the lift until.

Rama heard him and rode along, replying politely that he was only going a short distance. As he rode about 50 feet forward he stopped and rode back to them. He mentioned that the school was too far to walk, especially for the school kid. Without making any further enquiry he offered to provide them the lift to the school even though it was out of the way and his family was waiting for him as he only came out to pick up breakfast from a nearby tiffin centre.

The college age youngster mentioned that the kid was his nephew and he was visiting his grandparents the previous day. Rama dropped them both at the school gate, waited until they both entered the premises and then went about on his way home. He knew when he stopped, that it was really not a choice. He could not let the little boy walk to a far away school, on a summer morning amid an ongoing heat wave. What he had done would sure be called helping, but to Rama, there was really not any choice in what was done. There is no need to celebrate a gesture that is small or for that matter a big one.

A mother who has gone through the experience of childbirth, needs no explanation or incentive to help a child have a happy upbringing. It takes a lot to Live, but to deny a child a happy upbringing can potentially turn him into a monster of gargantuan proportions. Why? Because misery loves company. But, a mother can only do so much with the time and energy she has. Even though there is an ability to help more children, due to lack of financial and time-wise (FreeTime Freedom) freedom, there is a realistic limitation. Not just mothers, anyone can help when there is an ability along with the FreeTime Freedom.

You have to be free to be able to help. This cannot be overstated.

Maybe that's why freedom is such a highly valued tenet. Freedom doesn't just mean freedom to choose but freedom to truly be free. Free of tension, worry and apprehension. Not to mention, you can only be free to an extent, because no one will be able to honestly feed you forever for free.

In most cases the ability to help is not a problem while the availability, i.e., being free to help, the lack of FreeTime Freedom is a real obstacle.

To phrase it concisely, to be in a position to carry on the duty to help, which is not really a choice, one has to be time-wise free.

Unfortunately, a quick survey of a handful of people in a close vicinity will reveal the sad fact of an epidemic of people destined to a perpetual lack of time syndrome (PLTS), for anything meaningful. So, when so much help that should have otherwise been delivered is long overdue, it is bound to aggravate the problems.

The wise soul within Rama's mind explained, "When someone becomes so very desperate for intimacy, he would happily marry a whore", he continued, "such is the beast of man, when the hunger isn't assuaged in time, man unleashes the beast within. It's not pleasant when the streets of society are filled with such beasts". Rama pondered, "who is to say, we are not already there?".

Society's problems have become a favourite pastime. People laughing at each others' miseries is a true testament to the degree of decay achieved over the years. In its various forms, the newspapers, news channels, social media, etc. The disconnectedness monster has manifested its natural ugliness into glitz and glam on the outside and a manifestly rotten core on the inside.

To Help is God's work. God's work is more work than any artificial make-believe task list we keep calling work. In work, whether Patriotic, Personal or Professional - cannot be about enjoyment, because it must be about the duty one has toward the society.

Enjoyment must be limited to one's family and friends. Social enjoyment attracts the wrong perception of you from others. As they suffer on the inside, your public display of joy, though not directed at them, will be filed under "who is responsible for my misery ?" category.

Then arrived the twist in this story. Rama came back to Reality from the preponderance of thoughts occupying his mind. "All these thoughts of help are making my head hurt". His thoughts continued, "how can he possibly help ? He is after all a small man in the big scheme of things and contributing any help seemed beyond him". The wise soul within confirmed the notion to be true.

He said, "Life isn't about helping others but yourself. Efforts in this matter may seem like attempts to help others, but are helping you make and build or write things that you best use to help yourself", to which Rama responded with a sigh at the obviousness of the remark, " If I can't help myself, how can I possibly be trusted to help others". To help yourself is not really a choice but the very point of your existence. Shying away from the task is an inevitable prolonging of the status quo of suffering.

When Rama was helping by giving a lift earlier that morning, even in that exercise, he was helping himself become a better person. When faced with a decision to either do something, or walk away from the situation he could help with, he helped, and that in turn triggered in his mind a flurry of thoughts which went on to enrich his entire day.

To Help and to be Free are one and the same because you wouldn't be free if you hadn't helped yourself. To Help is to help become free from tension, worry and apprehension.

CHAPTER 11

MONEY BLANKET

Is a Tool, not a Solution

The ground you walk on could very well collapse under the weight of the burden you carry on your shoulders. Such is the challenge of life, but it doesn't always mean it's too heavy for you, it just means you need to start walking on stronger ground. The strength and the sturdiness of your morals will determine whether you will make it across. The Ground, in the phrase used, isn't literal. Your morals are the support system that you stand on.

Staying in a country in the northern hemisphere, Rama quickly learned the need for blankets. By this time it was also becoming clear that he very well may be residing in the real world but was rarely living in it. Most of his living time is spent in the cosiness and comfort of his mind. A pejorative way people use to casually and quite callously describe such a situation is, "Body Present, Mind Absent", but what was actually happening with Rama, was that his entire existence was becoming about being present in the mind, which is a far cry from the silly phrase.

Rama's mind went back to the thought of blankets. A role of a blanket, as generally understood, is that it keeps the cold away. Which very well may be a reasonable way of looking at it. But, we tend to forget that the blanket, more than preventing cold from coming in, keeps your body heat from escaping out. Blanket is only a tool that enhances your ability to survive, however, the underlying ability was already always within you. Life, too, is like that. We may sometimes have a reverse understanding of things.

The same is applicable to Life's Riches. Be it the Heat or Riches - they are already inside you. Money doesn't make you rich, it only keeps you from becoming poorer. Sure the blanket helps you, but only because you have the heat inside you. And just like that, sure the money helps you, but that's only because you have the ability to take care of yourself.

Unnecessary importance given to money is like respecting the blanket. No offence to the blanket, but a blanket doesn't give you the ability of inner heat, it is merely a tool that enhances it.

It's difficult for a lot of people to understand money, which is why it can get confusing to decide where to compromise and where not to.

If you compromise on your ability for the sake of money that would be a waste of your ability, because the money you earn is not going to be of any use in enhancing your abilities for whatever may come your way. Your abilities are given for purposes that are not always, as of yet, known.

Rama compared this to his then employment situation and whether his employment, for which he was being compensated in money, was enhancing his abilities, i.e., Life skills? The answer to it wasn't readily available with him. He took his time and so should others. Like most shortcuts, to define things it's much easier to start with thinking what they are not. "Is this the best use of his time ?", Rama thought. He went ahead as it at least provided some movement to his train of thought about his employment. Whether it was truly enhancing his Life skills, that are useful in truly freeing him and not just useful in landing another job.

The conditioning of the human mind seems to be such that a default state of a sane mind is to say no to all change, even though change is the only possible certainty pertaining to the way of life. To want to live, as if folks can just coast across life on an autopilot mode, facing no challenges whatsoever, is to live in a fool's paradise.

Modern Employment has become the master of promising the utmost stability of all other possible alternative ways of living. The very thought of a Stable life, something so antithetical and by far the most repugnant forms of life, has quickly become the most preferred choice and is causing quite a stir.

This reminded Rama of the meditation retreat he had attended a while back. Like the good student he thinks he is, on the fourth day of the course, when it was time for students to attempt a crucial level, he reached the state of peak awareness after some struggle. It was a state of body and mind so profound, which cannot be described in words. But, he also noticed that others weren't reaching the state.

As it was strictly forbidden to interact with others at the retreat, Rama went to the teacher and informed him of the path he took to achieve the level. He suggested that if the Teacher could inform this to all the students it can be very helpful to them.

Teacher very calmly and politely shared with Rama quite a pearl of wisdom. He stated that reaching this state is a journey that can transcend lifetimes and you are where you are because of who you are. All those who strive to achieve the level will achieve it in their own timelines.

Rama pondered whether the reason behind why so many people get trapped in the Money Blanket of Employment, trading their abilities for cash, probably has something to do with the journey of the soul that transcends lifetimes.

Falling in the Employment Trap is the second easiest way to earn another lifetime on the planet. Trapping others in Employment Traps is the easiest way to earn another lifetime on the planet. Doing things that don't make sense to you but only upon instruction is the way you get distracted away from the duty and purpose for which you took birth in the first place... paying off past life debts, atoning for the sins committed, etc.

Rama sees this journey as the purification of the Soul. This journey transcends lifetimes for a reason - because we're not ready until we're ready, and we're not done until we're done. Rama does not want another life. He wants salvation at the end of this one.

Unfortunately, the customs that govern the modern workplace frown upon their employees seeking salvation while on their payroll. Rules governing such violations are covered in the professional conduct section of employment contracts. Professional conduct is just a fancy term for Discipline. Asking fully grown adults to maintain discipline at workplace sounds childish and asinine, so other words were invented to convey the same meaning.

As Rama was doubting the preferred way of the majority of the World, it also didn't get lost on him that the majority of his countrymen are self employed, inadvertently doing God's work, preserving the sanity that's strongly holding the culture together.

Rama was taught that the way of life was to study well and get a job, where employers are picking you right out of the college campus to work at their companies and factories. Rama thought, "it appears that the setup may not be working in the interest of students".

Rama who has already been an employee for more than a decade has benefitted from the money he earned from working a job. However, there was a palpable sense of something lacking. This feeling very well could be imaginary and he was aware of that possibility. He fully understood that the roots of all problems are initially imagined and then they manifest their way out into reality.

As long as the problem idea stays in the mind, the problem, as simply as it can be imagined, can also be imagined away. But, once it leaves the mind, it cannot simply be imagined away. It needs to be solved. Such is the nature of our problems, they must be imagined away in the mind as much as possible and all others must be solved in the real world.

Rama studied not just his profession but also other professions to see if he can identify any useful patterns. In an increasingly mechanical professional routine, jobs can start to feel like prison sentences. You are only there because you are required to comply. Prolonged forced compliance programs will take the life out of the duty, leaving behind a metaphorical trained monkey incharge of a circus trick. This monkey is neither interested nor desires to leave, because it's tied to the leash named salary.

Some serious examples of the damage from job holders occurs when Doctors, Engineers and Lawyers start looking at their own family as patients, problems and clients, respectively. Ideally people in these noble professions must be looking even at outsiders as family members and provide them with the best professional solution possible, but, we see it happening in reverse, which defeats the point of the professions.

The need for highlighting these specific professions is because these are essential professions for any society to function properly. A casual, careless and an uncommitted attitude within professions can cause severe damage to the society as a whole. Other professions also fall prey to this behaviour. A real estate developer will start sizing up his family members' net worth based on the potential for development of their property ownership share.

While all of the above behaviour is bad for society, not a single voice is being raised at increasing awareness about the ill effects of spillover of professional conduct into personal lives.

Rama attributes such behaviour with the disconnectedness that has crept into the education system. Education which is supposed to bring students closer to society, so they can contribute with full conscience, is instead stuffing them in cubicles far removed from it.

The wise soul within Rama is watching all these thoughts in his mind closely and curiously to see whether Rama will reach out to him or will he attempt to figure things out on his own. He knows that Rama is on the right track and struggling but nevertheless stands by him, as his beloved pupil is learning the ways of the world.

Rama is perplexed, seeing how in the matter of employment, which he clearly is dissatisfied with, has no choice but to continue on because he is bound by duty to those bound to him, and depend on him for basic survival. He is torn to apply his recent revelation about how helping oneself is not really a choice but a duty, and how it could very well become the defining purpose of his life. To be duty bound to himself and leave his employment in order to help himself.

All the efforts to help himself in this regard are turning his own against him like a pack of blood hungry wolves. Not to mention others who are ready to pounce on the slightest chance. Rama's journey of hiding behind the shadows, which he wouldn't wish upon his harshest critics, is not one of stability. It is at least consistent with the proper way to live, so Rama is finding it hard to complain about his circumstances.

Even though he hasn't yet found a way out of his predicament, he believes he is in the right direction and is also sure to be on the right side of history, on this question of the forever employment situation of all humans everywhere.

Rama is thinking about reaching out to the Wise Soul within and discussing with him on the topic. He hears the voice, "hello friend, I was thinking about reaching out to you too".

Rama thinks, "is this a choice I'm faced with?" and whatever Rama thinks, it gets heard by the Wise Soul within as it happens. If it's help that's required from me, even if it is unto myself, it cannot be a choice, but is rather a duty. Duty is not a choice with options, but a decision with a simple yes or no answer. Either you decide to take action or you don't.

The wise soul within is enjoying this self discovery of Rama and he wants in. The Wise Soul also starts thinking in a way audible to Rama, much like his inner voice, but it's not just an inner voice, it is the wisdom of the Soul.

To decide is not about choices, but about action. A truly conscientious individual may be faced with a thousand decisions before every step he takes. But such is the burden of life of such individuals. Yet, they walk through life as if floating in the wind. To that person a thousand decisions are all about moving in the same direction, the direction guided by their moral compass.

An example to differentiate between a choice and a decision, is that of the contemporary phenomenon generally known as social media, where people also exist in a virtual reality with a vague resemblance to the physical one.

With an increasing connectedness to the virtual world than to the real - the world along with its inhabitants is getting sucked into the cyber sphere ever so fast. The basic need for survival and the means to sustain oneself, people are reshaping themselves in the image of this new world.

With our naturally evolved senses unable to work in the virtual sphere, the world may have become even more vicious than before. People are being left defenceless against an onslaught of lies and deception. Whether to post or not is a choice. This choice is as meaningless as writing on water. The decision is whether to act or not on said post.

All tech solutions are becoming about how to fake it rather than owning what is. Social media is entertainment, not a solution to your problems. The filters, the backgrounds, the themes and others couldn't be more telling if they tried. Faking, lying, cheating, as it seems, has become justifiable if someone's survival depends on it. This was always the norm since the beginning of time, so, let's not fool ourselves and call this progress. The decision to fake, cheat and lie, as it seems, is being covered in Social Media 101 right there in kindergarten alongside the alphabets. All of this is causing suffering.

A soul with love and friendliness to other souls in proximity to itself will not allow pain and suffering to occur, but it happens because there are no such things as love or friendship. The fact these non existent phenomenons are taking a huge chunk of our time is disconcertingly distracting from the real solutions, if there are any.

CHAPTER 12

LOVE & FRIENDSHIP

both replaced with Life, in usage.

As there is no such thing as friendship, it would be worth, at this point, to expand on that topic a bit more, thought Rama. Along with Friendship, people are best served to also understand that there is no Love. Friendship, as it is understood, exists between people, if there is some business between them. Exactly like that, Love, as it is understood, can only exist between people, if the bonding of Life exists between them.

Overuse of these words has thrust upon them a sort of romance and thereby have become respected and revered as totally legitimate constructs. Many, without fully understanding the dark side of these constructs tend to get lost in the definitions and expectations.

He told himself, "Listen carefully Rama, He who knows you, owns you; He who thinks and acts like he owns you, must surely already know you". That's not even the interesting part, as interesting as it is. "If you don't know yourself, you are up for grabs for anyone with a little bit of trickery up their sleeve". "Know yourself, before you even think of knowing the smallest factoid about another".

A Nation full of people, who barely know themselves, are prime for picking and that is the story of the country. The wide-spread voluntary human trafficking of children by their own parents must become a cautionary tale for all those nations who have forgotten themselves for a plate of meal. All in the name of these 2 words that don't even really exist. They have come to fill the void created by ignorance of self with flowery ideas of finding oneself in them. Which is precisely why, these 2 words must be discouraged from usage in common parlance. With the interests of the people in mind, this can be done by revealing the Truth.

There is no Love, there is no Friendship, there is only Life.

All those whom you "love" and are "friends" with will remain in your Life as you will have a life with them. An application of this rule would be the replacement of the fake 3 words, with a genuinely meaningful 4 words, "You are My Life". You can imagine saying these 4 words to anyone close to you and it immediately makes sense. The word Life has an inbuilt accountability and a zero tolerance to bull waste. Life constitutes everything from the smallest feeling to the biggest event. It's not something you ask for but is rather given to you because it'll take you on a journey, a journey that can only be experienced.

Rama understood that it'll take time for those that aren't ready to change old habits. Some people may have defined their entire lives around friendships. If you don't think about it in depth, "Friendship" however it is understood, can be a truly life making addition. In a world that is becoming increasingly isolated, it's unwise to deliberately lose friends. A life without friends, however misunderstood the concept maybe, is no fun. Even when it's only for business it's a good way to maintain social interactions, man being a social animal and all.

Accepting that discouraging the usage of the word "Friendship" might not be worth the trouble, Rama's ready to make a deal on discouraging the usage of the word "Love" and be instead replaced with "Life". "Love" targets the young when they are most vulnerable, it must be dealt with swiftly and strongly. Seminars may be conducted about the lack of understanding and misinterpretation of the word. The cheesy movies based on Love may be rated A/C/AG for Adult, Comedy & Absolute Garbage.

Rambha, Urvashi & Menaka were, are and will always be distractions. Rama can spend a long time thinking about distractions, but that would become too self explanatory. Love has become a major distraction. For a non-existent entity it is creating a lot of problems for the people because they are using it as a drug. Like a super drug with a hope that it solves everything. Like it is the silver bullet solution for all the ills of the world. When someone says, "Love is the Language of the World", or "Love is the Solution" they are not just lying, they are selling, and probably for a good profit, do not fall for it.

CHAPTER 13

DEBUNKING

the Masters' Work

Rama has arrived at the point where it's time to debunk the Masters' work. He picks up the pen and starts writing.

To follow one's heart was the main message of all the books he had read. To follow your heart and to fight for what you believe are not exactly the same thing, except in the few cases when it is. But, also understand that you will be punished for following your heart by all those who aren't. This is natural and to be expected. Mob mentality and group survival will try and prevent any opposing points of views or ways of life. To learn about the denial of this truth to the readers of the books was disappointing.

The impression given that there is a universal force that pushes us in the right direction does seem to be right, but it's more likely that unsuspecting youngsters with immature brains and a naive approach to the world, are typically fooled into some distraction that feeds some self serving interest of somebody else but his own.

According to Rama, a writer doesn't write to solve the world's problems. He writes in a desperate attempt to solve his own. But, what if, in a particular written work, he doesn't solve the problem? Who picks up the slack on this brave contribution of making things worse for all? A Writer writes for himself. His personal journey to save himself will pave the path that will add to efforts that may save others, but being only about serving others isn't, wasn't and should never be how one lives their life.

Being the change you wish to see in the world, is a nice sounding line that distracts the individual from saving himself. This line was and still is never fully explained and perhaps for some undisclosed reason.

Unless one is indoctrinated to feel like he exists to help others, as his purpose of life, he may be unwilling to let others force him into a life of serving self-serving Wolves. Wolves who already know the higher truth and use it to their advantage but never share it with others, because this affects their comfort zone of using others to get their things done.

Just like there are no public discussions of the ill effects of video games; to expect retrospective studies analysing the damage done from a particular literary piece or a movie, is futile. There is nobody watching out for others, because each is busy spinning the wheel like a mouse in a trap. Books get published, movies get made and wealth gets accumulated and there ends that story.

The risk-reward dynamic runs counter to the hard work philosophy taught to the kids. High Risk - High Reward, only works because it's an unfair world. Your ability to risk, getting into danger, shows the unseen paths, allowing a sort of shortcut to success. However, the propensity, ability to risk and other virtues needed to insulate oneself from the consequences of risk, have nothing to do with any of the virtues that are taught as being needed for success. If it were in the open, that one can only succeed if they take risks, kids would not be sent circling the fake rosy path of success through hard work. Instead, they would be trained on how to take risks properly.

Be it in comedy, entertainment or any other form of work that engages people, you either take them to a higher level with you or you take them lower. It can be a thousand times more difficult to take people higher while it being a cake walk to drag them to a lower level. It's not hard to imagine which way is sought more often than not. If you are not the smartest person in the room on a particular topic, you have no business making statements or producing content. And, if you are, and are not actively involved in making statements and producing content, you are wasting your talents behind the desk.

This is how things should work, but no, this is not how it's happening. Somebody plants an unrealistic notion in the mind at a very young age that they should follow their heart. This happens way before the child even understands what a heart is and why it might have desires. He is typically already halfway through on this path, before he can even think to question it.

It's not the heart that's taking the man or his mind on a merry-go-round. It's all these ideas that were indoctrinated at such young ages that are causing all the troubles. Ideas such as becoming a musician or an artist or a doctor or a lawyer or, the mass favourite - the saviour of peoples, are causing a lot of suffering.

Not a single person, in the school years, inculcates in the young mind the idea of knowing thy self and then understanding their true nature of their existence. How can one be useful to others without knowing himself first ?! He can't.

The wise soul said, "this is an important lesson to learn. To not be carried away by life's fantasies and be true to oneself".

Rama thought, the wise soul teaches some serious lessons and some not so serious, but there are no lessons that are small or big. The weight of a lesson gets attached to it on how useful it has been to you and how useful it can be going forward.

When a person, going about his life wants to self assess, there is a thumb rule that can be put to use. Are you decluttering or are you nonsense? Every direction you accidentally lay your eyes on is laced with a plethora of distractions. In the chaos that's being thrown at folks, your contribution must declutter the nonsense not amplify it.

This may not be obvious to an untrained eye, but one who has mastered Life can breathe without any anxiety and go about his day with peace, because he knows that things always add up.

It may seem like they don't because you are missing an angle. Let's take a trend that is considered a problem and needs correcting. The next generation don't want to get married. It is because they have no support system and therefore blaming them is pointless. The fact it reached this point means that the seeds that are reaping this crop were laid a longtime ago. Seeking an instant solution will not work.

Shaming or forcing people to get married, so the society can sustain itself will not work. But, what will work is to identify the seeds from the past and device a corrective mechanism and lay new seeds that will potentially correct the problem, before the damage done is too much to recover from. Sometimes it can take centuries for a damage to be repaired and a wrong to be corrected. If something is taking too long to correct, be of the attitude that the collective consciousness is working on more important things.

The problem lies with the attitude that starts its day to find problems to solve. This is a problem, that is a problem, everything is a problem. People are the problem, politicians are the problem, parties are the problem, courts are the problem. None of these are problems, they are just facts making up our reality. If you can't square things for people, it's most likely because it's someone else's duty to square with them.

What may seem like a problem with this line of thinking is that if nothing is a problem, then there is nothing to solve. No one has to lift a finger and all things will forever be happy. Which is not what is being said here at all. Things will add up when all investigations are properly done, and the root cause is identified. This process will require people to dig deep and not just give things a whitewash.

Additionally, a "things always add up attitude", is one of positive vibrations, it tempers our judgement of others and keeps things friendly.

The exercise doesn't stop until all things related to the thing you are thinking about add up, even after double and triple verifications. The solution to address the root cause once devised, upon mere opening of eyes, the root cause will start to mend itself. Soon it'll become clear that it only existed because no one ever bothered to take a good look at it.

Things always add up because they went through the hellfire of reality and beat all odds to become part of the existing reality. All other possibilities may sound better only because the full picture has not yet been considered. Things always add up and will never add up to zero. Life always thrives and such is its blessing.

CHAPTER 14

THE PHILOSOPHY

of Family

When Rama says, "once people start appreciating the finer things in life, there is no going back from that", most people can understand it. But, what isn't so well established is that "finer things" can mean totally different things to different people. Family can become the finest thing for all, with nothing more than a quick attitude fix.

Ultimately, Kartavyam is about the family, it's your contribution to the Universe. Your desire may or may not come from it, but it sure will go to it. No Kartavyam can sever one from one's family, because that severance negates any personal ambition. Individual ambition with no consideration of the family will be harmful for both the entity and the family.

If you can't see that, what's good for your child is good for you, and what's good for you is good for your child, no one can help you.

What's good for the family is good for all its members and also the other way around. But, the harsh truth you learn the harshest way is that everything you believe to be absolutely true is wrong... not because you are wrong per se, but in comparison with the truth you don't know, you might as well settle.

You thought the belief instilled in you at a young age that it's best to raise your kids with their grandparents was true. Which it very well could be, but, what if the grandparents don't want to raise your kids, in that they believe it may no longer be in their best interest to do it. They'll show you the hell for asking them what they don't want to be part of. In case when the grandparents are so saintly that they are basically breaking themselves apart in catering to family needs, the Universe will step in, and give you a couple knocks on your head to correct the course you are on and stop making them suffer. This particular problem is totally avoidable with timely marriages, where the grandparents would not be too old to be present in the lives of their own grandchildren.

Now, how do you walk away from what you have worked to lock yourself in? You can't. Queue double suffering for yourself because your kids will also unleash their wrath on you. Perhaps deservedly so, for putting them in that position.

A scientific way of looking at a family would be that they all share the same DNA. There is a tangible way of proving that these people didn't just randomly get together. There are reports that are talking about the memory storing ability of a single gram of DNA being 215 Petabytes. That is a lot of storage for such a small mass.

The burden of DNA memory. We may have only just found out that it can be used to store information, but what about what is already in its storage. The genetic characteristics, the rhyme, the rhythm, the height, the weight and the looks are obvious, but what about Karma? Is our DNA carrying our karma in it? Might the log record of our deeds, not be somewhere in some book in another world, but within us in each of our cells.

How then in the passing of this DNA from parents to children, the offspring has a different karma than their parents? Do we know that it is different, for sure? It may be different but perhaps not by a lot. And, what about the soul? What is its connection to the DNA and with the Karma of the person?

This is the first time for Rama, when the nature of our Soul and its role are becoming a bit clearer. The assignment of a soul to a body, is also perhaps not an outside job, but could very much be an internal mechanism. Rama didn't think anything when he was repeatedly being told that God was within us, but to imagine that the entire mechanism that is running humanity and perhaps the Universe was always within us, was eye opening.

Rama recalls from the Geetha that all the souls were once part of Paramatma, and that they eventually reach Paramatma again. In the limited understanding and wisdom Rama interprets as, the Souls are being born and reborn as part of procreation, but these souls are not always starting from the very beginning, but from where they have left off in their previous journey.

This is how closely families are bound. The parent and the grandparent souls, apart from providing nourishment, also nurture the child souls to move further in their journey by teaching them what they have learnt in their lives.

Coming back to the burden of DNA memory. Salvation is the destination, Family is the vehicle. This journey must be recorded in the DNA.

Meditation teachers say that it took Buddha several lifetimes until he finally attained Salvation. All your work must enable you to become non-reacting to the stimulus. For which you are first required to learn to focus on your breathing, observe all sensations and accept that all matter is just vibrations and all these vibrations are all impermanent. All sensations, all pain and all joy, all impermanent. You will observe and let it go, because it's all impermanent and then there is no sensation that can bother you. That is what it means to lose all desire and that is when you won't come back and have another life.

Rama exercises caution here because "losing all desire toward life" can be the easiest thing to misinterpret. To not misinterpret is the challenge within itself. Whenever there is an idea that is so appealing, it behoves one to at least try it out. This idea from someone or someplace else, appealed to Gautama, or, it might be that Gautama figured the idea out and shared it with the world. Because, that's what the greats among us do, share the good with everyone, so the effect of bad becomes a little less.

The family can be the world family, the Vasudaika Kutumbam. Like the drops of river that are flowing, a drop splits into more drops. It doesn't mean the resulting water drop is lesser, it's still water, it's the same water. The small water particle somehow knows to use the hydrogen and oxygen available to it and make more water. A baby may be created physically smaller but it'll grow up. Both parents and the children continue their lives being fully alive. Life creates more life, and it continues to live on.

It is quite complicated to understand how the child carries on with his own journey to salvation, but what about the salvation of the parent?

If we are all part of the same source soul, shouldn't the salvation of one be the salvation of all? It's logically not, because we are all still longing, we are all still suffering. The journey of an individual soul continues forward, regardless of the source of the soul.

There must be a mechanism or an explanation that I'm missing, thought Rama.

Per conventional wisdom, there are 7 lives for each before they can attain salvation, there is reincarnation from Life 1 to Life 7 and perhaps a choice to choose the next life or maybe they just wait their turn. A cycle of Grandparents and parents reincarnating as children and grand children until their 7th Life. And, when there is no grandparent or parent there to reincarnate, it's possible that another soul who doesn't have a child or grandchild to reincarnate could take birth as an offspring of someone closer; or a new soul in its first life would be created as an offspring to those with no parents and grandparents awaiting; or it could be any other infinite possibilities where the soul can mature.

With this said, the father could very well be a lower life number and his son in his last life. The typical father and son frequency mismatch is probably because of the reverse seniority. The Son is actually older in Life number, even though the father is physically older in the number of Birthdays. Rama thought this makes sense. There would be little frequency mismatch between family members when a new 1st life gets created or when both the parent and child, both understand and appreciate the cycle of life.

So, when you see a family that gets along so well and you feel left out, just understand that these maybe the simpler times before life gets all exciting for them too... perhaps a few years down the line when the souls rotate back into the family.

The karma of the past lives gets stored in the DNA, and it starts where it left off. Perhaps there is also a points system on who gets a priority when there are multiple souls waiting.

The easiest and the most effective way to reach 7th life is with your family. The life experience one has to go through in these 7 lives can be pretty consistent through and through, so long as the family values are kept intact.

When there is a consistent family life as part of the journey, the soul can focus on attaining the maturity it takes to join the Paramatma, one life at a time.

This sounds like the most perfect reason to protect one's family and strengthen its values.

There is just one more thing missing... the karma balance would keep changing until the last breath, so how does that DNA memory transfer into that of a newborn. This one Rama still hasn't figured out. "Maybe there is a transmission mechanism from one member to another in order to transfer pertinent data. But, just knowing where I'm going with this feels fantastic", thought Rama, as he wrote on.

No one can know what their life number is, except perhaps when it is 7. Because knowing that it's any other number than 7 could potentially have a reverse effect. There is just no way to know. You can imagine yourself to be any life number and observing the life experiences can perhaps paint a decent picture of where you might be.

Rama thought that he would be pleased to learn that he has convinced even one person, using the above theory, that the protection of one's family is paramount not only for the purposes of survival but also in the context of Salvation. Rama would like this theory, which by all means is a combination of various concepts of reincarnation, seven lives and salvation to be known as "The Philosophy of Life" or "The Theory of Life", and the one who understands it will also understand, that no one ever needs any outside help to attain moksha.

There is a lot of talk about the purpose of life but what about the responsibility, the onus, after all that is the name of the book, Kartavyam - Onus Upon Us. Generally speaking, the onus is upon the parents to teach the children, because they are older and therefore responsible. But, now that we can understand the possibility of a son being older in Life Number, the responsibility must lie on the elder.

A Son, with an older life number, not because he knows it for sure, but because he can sense it, must not shirk away from his Kartavyam. Life number is not going to mean anything if he doesn't take responsibility. Such are the challenges. These are not straight forward, walk-the-line and win-the-prize, kind of contests. These are, figure-things-out-yourself, take-action-and-attain-Salvation, kind of contests.

The taking of responsibility cannot be limited only to those from the family but also all others. Those who are able to sense they are older, in life number, should stop complaining and take control of their own lives. Instead of blaming teachers, who are just following orders and not really helping their students grow, the person who notices it must do his part, not by badmouthing those responsible, but by correcting the situation to the extent he can.

CHAPTER 15

SIMPLER WAY

if it's not, you maybe doing something wrong

Rama realised that he had been spending a lot of time in his mind. He was physically meeting all his expectations in the real world, in a more or less auto-pilot mode. In one such phase, under the influence of an inspiring book, he had missed the entire social media spring. He only learned about the massive appeal it had garnished in the world much later. Since he had not been part of the spring, he didn't get its appeal and just as quickly went back to living in his mind.

The memories of the journey one takes from 1st Life to the 7th life are not accessible during the lifetimes, but the journey that occurs in the current life is inescapable. The journey is perhaps as real as it gets for someone. Its harshness goes about moulding the person inside and out.

Rama himself is going through this journey, of sometimes literal travel to places and change of professions. In his journey, Rama felt that his journey wasn't real while at his profession. He was far removed from any inner workings of companies he was with. He couldn't discern any core meaning, except for the superficial and obvious utilitarian purpose they seem to be serving.

It felt like he was doing something wrong. It wasn't getting any simpler and was surely getting more and more complicated by the day. But Rama, the stalwart optimist he was, opined, "just because I maybe doing something wrong doesn't mean it's the wrong thing to do. It was just wrong for me to do it, yet nevertheless be useful, valuable and feel like the right thing for others at the receiving end". Also, it helped him gain a livelihood for his daily needs until he could sustain himself by doing the right thing in a simpler way.

Whenever he could, he chose a different profession where he can "do new things everyday", which, incidentally, were also the exact words Rama believes that God Krishna himself told him in a dream just as he woke up one morning.

The time had come when Rama had to end his journey of the distant lands. He was able to extrapolate into the future, based on his present. He passionately wanted his future to be in his motherland, to which he had never, not for one moment, disconnected.

Rama thinks up the story of the Seed and the Soil, where the Soil starts to think that there are too many trees and therefore decides, based on the virtue of being the birther, nourisher and the sole place holder of life, it doesn't need anymore seed, and cuts off all new seeds from being sown.

Soil, being the observer it is, thinks the bees pollinate, fruits fall, the birds drop and the forests grow. They do. But, the Soil forgot that it was being narrow-minded.

The forests may seem to grow without the need for the seed, while completely ignoring the role of seeds and everyone else. It happens because the seeds that make new plants, trees, flowers, fruits, bees and birds haven't decided so abruptly to cut off all new seeds from being sown.

The seed should not think that it can grow trees in thin air, nor should the soil think it can grow the trees on its own. They are both parts of the same whole where each is incomplete without the other. To deny this is akin to saying that you want to enjoy the fruits and survive on the life it brings you, but you refuse to acknowledge the cross pollination that is responsible for the fruit.

Before Rama moved on from the significance of the DNA, and the burden of its memory capabilities, he wanted to acknowledge another angle of human evolution and its progress, as can be evidenced in our DNA... In the story of Bhaktha Prahalada, the devotee was saved by God Vishnu from his own father, who was a demon king. The story comes from a different yuga, where the Angels and Demons were physically different people and each had their own worlds they inhabited. There would be clashes between the two groups in their aspirations to control the 3 worlds. One might call these as the Simpler times.

But, as time progressed, the game, so to speak, entered a higher level. Now both the Angels and Demons share the same human form. One can try and understand the turmoil of his enemy, but to comprehend this constant internal turmoil as the perpetual state of modern human society is not one for the faint hearted. A parent, based on his life experiences can become a saint, while the offspring could turn into a monster owing to his own experiences. The opposite could be just as equally possible.

In the current level of evolution, where the good and the evil are both within the same human form, killing off your enemy is no longer an allowed form of survival principle. It would be a waste of enormous proportions to simply kill off an opponent. No one who can truly appreciate life and its journey can even fathom the commission of such a horrendous act.

"Even more importantly, our Life was never about others. One's journey to Salvation cannot be obstructed by others even if they tried. All other forms of opposition and enmity are just distractions trying to pull you away from your road to salvation", Rama told himself.

The purpose of life is Moksha alone. The enemy lies within, who owing to the primal instincts, desires and weaknesses, wants to hold on to life.

An interesting view point to consider, when you open your eyes and look at all the billions of souls traversing the planet, is that there must be a whole lot of those who are in their 7th life, getting ready to reach salvation. You don't look at them with hope, because their journeys have nothing to do with yours. You look at them with curiosity and how they conduct themselves in comparison with others of potentially lower life numbers.

Rama begins to correlate his thought train with the Truth. Will they sync up and go in the same direction or will they crash into each other ?

There is not just one hard truth. There cannot be. To force billions of people into constrained pathways and pushing them through, will result in large scale suffering. A path one takes in his life, must not affect the path of others, as they don't have to be connected. It's easier that way. This way is not just the way of Life but is their path to enlightenment. Each individual, in his own way, at his own pace, will figure things out.

To find one's own truth is perhaps the greatest definition of it.

When someone is in their 1st life, it doesn't mean that they are immature, it means they are the closest to Paramatma. As they were only just created from the Paramatma into this life. The qualities, the freshness and the purity of the Paramatma are so near and are able to provide guidance and solid foundation for the reunification journey.

Rama thinks that the 4th life is the most difficult life, because that is when the soul has come the furthest from the Paramatma since its creation. After which it starts to go closer to the Paramatma again.

What's the first thing one does, when he is made aware of an important esoteric concept? They'll try and emulate it and then soon after they'll try and hack it to find some shortcut.

When someone has learned in passing that it is in fact Moksha that is the purpose of life, but they don't truly understand the meaning of the word, it creates commotion. Some may think Salvation means the end of life. A few people will interpret it to their convenience and make a wrong choice. A few others who may consider themselves well read and think that if you produce offspring, you are inevitably extending the suffering. which is indeed worse than previous understandings.

Someone before Rama has said, half knowledge is worse than ignorance. Put to rest all the ideas that if you don't have kids, you wont come back for another life. You will have salvation only when you reach the 7th life and have cleared all your karmic balance.

In this process and while on this journey, you may realise that in convincing another is when you can truly convince yourself; and also never forgetting that trusting an outsider more than you trust someone on the inside is the stupidest thing ever to do. Rama told to himself, "no one ever said that this was going to be easy".

CHAPTER 16

REVERSE PSYCHOLOGY

Is a heavy handed propaganda tool

Rama thinks that it is in our nature to emulate, but it's also natural to get hungry. Just because someone is hungry, it doesn't make it also natural for them to emulate stealing from another, to satisfy their hunger. To emulate others must be done so with extreme caution. All energies will be expended to get you to either emulate outside behaviour or react to it. This can be a trap.

It's not your duty to mirror others, but to perform your duty. It may include for you to listen, care and help as you can. Even though it's natural to feel compassion, it's not okay to mirror outside emotion in order to feel the connection. To watch a movie and mindlessly follow a certain behaviour, is the classic propaganda machine at work. We have all fallen for this trick. Modern propaganda has reached Inception levels of sophistication.

Sometimes, one may end up speaking the exact opposite words of what they mean, in order to get the response they seek. Words matter and meaning behind those words matters even more. However, the most important are the actions that follow and the change they bring about. In the pursuit of this goal, whether one employs straight-talk or reverse psychology becomes secondary. One may often prefer straight-talk for its simplicity, but one must not be ignorant that the other option might be more effective.

All propaganda rides on exploiting basic human insecurities. A Man's weaknesses are what others are hell bent on finding out. All the "donate now" campaigns employ this technique. Make you experience it by showing the experience. It can be very effective for the campaigner, but to allow the mirroring of the experience within you, as natural as it may feel, can mean a heavy personal, and at times financial, toll.

Some of these images and video content can stay with people forever. Doing a brief research before consuming the content can help filter, unsavoury, semi-permanent or permanent memory burns.

If you think you can hide your weaknesses, you are better off to resolve strongly and rid yourself of all your weaknesses. Weaknesses will be found and be exploited to their fullest extent. To believe in the goodness of mankind and trusting of everyone must start and end with yourself. Even if you end up trusting someone who seems like he is the most genuine and the kindest hearted person, chances are that they were already compromised and they don't even know it. Trusting is risky business. There is simply not enough bandwidth in the modern day lifestyles, to really get to know someone to the level of trusting them.

To carefully analyse a person's qualities, strengths, weaknesses, training, education and then form a solid opinion about whether someone is trustworthy, can take years. Rama hasn't conducted a sample study but the probability suggests that if this were a test, at least half the people will fail it, for trusting without testing.

This is not to suggest that the world is unfair and untrustworthy, but to stress that Life is quite complex. To think that there isn't a hungry Lion around the corner, waiting to devour your ignorance, would only be making it too easy for the Lion.

Rama pauses for a second and tries to collect his thoughts, "what does reverse psychology have to do with reincarnation?"

Like the next man, Rama also fell in the trap set up by the barrage of propaganda the people are being subjected to. In order to comprehend even a little of what's being presented, one not only needs to rise above the propaganda, but also be fully present for the challenges he will face. It's not a single battle in which you win and you are set for the rest of your life.

A child is born with equal parts good and evil. In the child's life journey, within the internal fight between the good and the evil, whichever wins in that moment, becomes in charge of the soul for that moment. The incharge entity will try to make as much impact in its favour. This will affect the Karma account balance. The fight continues on, into the next moment.

Another such fight could be... You teach your children how to talk and they grow up to argue with you. You think they are ungrateful. But, they can only learn through argument, so that should be ok. And, in arguing with your children, you may also learn, correct and grow.

When the good wins, no one will ever notice it. Good gets done and that's that. But when the evil wins the fight, it becomes incharge and drives the family apart, wastes as much time as it can and prevents any good from coming out of the moment.

It is a zero sum game that only you are playing. Only you stand to gain or lose. Your impact on others is a bi-product, which won't add any positive karma balance unless it helps you advance your journey.

Everyone gets a fair shot at the game, in the most elaborate fashion with several second chances. Most importantly, everyone wins, just not all at the same time. Because everyone is from the same soul and winning is when they rejoin it. Lives are like physical exercise and activity, the creation of the soul from the Paramatma and its rejoining back is just part of a healthy life. Except, in this context it is of a much bigger life, the life of the Paramatma himself.

Since not all situations are discernible whether they are complex tests wrapped in a bunch of traps or they are pure innocence of life that inspires magical experiences, one could apply reverse psychology and decipher it better. It can also be an effective tool you can employ to get yourself out of a jam or hit the nail on the coffin of a challenge you face.

For reverse psychology to work, the most important qualifier is ego. If the person you want to use reverse psychology doesn't have an ego, you are out of luck, because it won't work. One without ego can take each situation by itself, for its own merits and make a decision. But when someone does have an ego, they will most likely fall prey to this technique.

Rama likes to consider himself to be one with no ego issues. He has seen and been through enough situations to understand it. There will still be many psy-ops that will be used by several entities for serving self interest or subvert opposition. People will fall for psy-ops because we are basically emotional beings, and are practically waiting to react. A right push of calculated and emotionally charged inputs can compromise an individual to the core. Beware!

Chapter 17
Parents

Are always on a Timeline

Once you have become a parent, you are always on a timeline. The needs of your children can't wait for you to take a long time off. The clock starts ticking from the moment you turn away from them. It's not an easy responsibility. It's no wonder so many parents are so bad at it. It can get frustrating, and the children, the perfect little sponges they are, pick up and absorb every little detail.

The otherwise free spirit, becomes then bound by his own love toward his offspring. From the sheer amount of time the kids spend with their parents, it'll be quite hard to imagine that they are not exact photocopies of their parents. Not just in genetics, but in behaviour, the way they walk, talk and all other things that make up a person's personality.

Parenting is not just about watching your kids as they grow upright, but to raise them right, to nurture them, whatever their nature may be. There aren't many problems in this world that couldn't have been addressed by parenting, Rama thought. Excuses with names such as work, business, passion, etc., that come in between the parent and his child are inexcusable. The compensation or reward one may gain from said efforts, won't even be close to the cost of the opportunities lost.

For example, when a child comes up to his father and asks him, "whether he should lie in order to get a job", the father then replies to him in only a few moments, "not to lie".

At that moment, whether the suggestion was right or not, is beyond the scope here. But the fact that it wasn't used to have a significant conversation a child gets to have with this father in his life, is the opportunity lost. Whatever may be the reason for the father to just give a quick answer to a question, be it work, business, passion or just good old laziness, the opportunity of a lifetime to teach something significant was lost forever. Because, an important question is seldom asked twice.

Parents must understand that they are always on a timeline and when it comes to the proper care and nurturing of their children, everything must be judged against the limited time and opportunities they have with them, and may aspire to never lose an opportunity to be there for their children when they need them the most.

Taking care of your wife, is taking care of your children. Taking care of your children is taking care of your wife. Likewise, taking care of your Wife and Children is taking care of your Parents and Grandparents, and taking care of your parents and grandparents is taking care of your wife and children. Because, in Family unity hides the Magic of Life that makes the World go around. In each moment, either this magic happens or there is suffering that takes its place.Taking care of yourself, is taking care of them both and everyone else who might ever need your caretaking. Neglecting individual members of your family is akin to neglecting your entire family, because they are closely connected.

Families must do the right things and have the right values for them to succeed. The biggest reason why families may be failing, despite seemingly best efforts, could be that there are no right values behind these efforts. One can't expect families to succeed just because they are forced to be together.

Families can be distant but still be strong when the underlying values are right and strong.

Marriages in families suffer because the families are suffering. Families are like Crop Cultivation. The seeds must be good, the manure must be organic, the soil must be rich and it needs the right amount of water along with constant care and affection towards the crop.

A Family by definition can never fail. They may suffer from time to time due to the lack of right values. The sheer act of sticking together is what will prevent failure. Which is why, if a family suffers, the answer is never to break away from it. Because, once you break away, not only will you continue to suffer, as the issue of lack of right values was never addressed, but you will have also dramatically increased your chances of failure, by removing yourself from the support of its immune system.

Giving credit where it's due, one of the inspiring books has done a decent job in conveying this dynamic between the parent and the child. Even though the episode was quite succinct, the author used the opportunity to make the conversation impactful. The father had a discussion on the topic, he questioned the choice of his child, and then went onto helping the child pursue his choice.

The world is perfect and fair and all that good stuff, and the only ones imperfect are us. How much one may prepare themselves for life that awaits them, it's more than likely that those we consider our own, are going to judge us the hardest on how poorly we fared. You teach your children how to talk and they grow up to argue with you, Rama recalled a thought from before.

When we can't always have, as much, in-person quality time with the children, other alternatives may be employed, which have its own advantages.

The parent may choose to write letters. Written word may often prove itself better than a speech, because more work goes into preparing it. A speech from a written word is even better, because an already better work is further improved by making it precise, witty, funny and captivating, so the speech can deliver the most impact.

Parents are practically falling apart attending to the needs of their children. Bodies aching, stomachs growling and heads banging. The parents of the modern day have the toughest responsibility of them all. The next time you see a parent, help them out if you can, but certainly make sure you don't waste their time as they are always on a timeline.

Chapter 18

7 LIVES

or 7 stages of life

A famous Telugu poet ends all his 4-line poems with the same last line. Rama has interpreted this 4th line to mean, "World is God, listen carefully". To view God as being within you is an outside-in world view, and to view yourself as being within God is an inside-out view. Rama is of the impression that those who think they are on this planet to chill, and don't have any purpose they need to fulfil, couldn't be more wrong about their perception of Life.

7 lives could very well be 7 stages of life that you must clear to win the Game of Life. If you are already on the 7th life, you slack off and don't clear the level or your karmic balance, you are coming back for more lives until it's all cleared.

It's like going to a buffet and you serve yourself food onto your plate. You are looking at all the varieties of food and taking more and more, without being mindful of what's already on your plate. The condition is that you may leave the restaurant only after finishing all the food on your plate. The more the food the longer it'll take. Metaphorically speaking, wiser choices such as yogurt are recommended to help with digestion. Food intake must be about sustenance. It's not easy, and it's about balance and moderation. Rama thinks that if it isn't challenging, it's probably not worth playing.

It has become quite evident to Rama that he is not just living an ordinary life. He is not one to sign up to follow instructions. In this regard, he is like the main characters of the inspiring books. Rama was like this, even before he ever read the books, so he couldn't blame the books for it.

Rama is not standing in front of a mirror, he is merely looking at the world outside. He is looking at all these people who have started behind him and have seemingly gone past him. He is trying to find himself in the journeys of others. The world of mirrors can only show him in a comparison with others. Someone's bigger car makes Rama look smaller, was the nature of thoughts running through his mind. This is Rama's alter ego who manifests from time to time.

His alter ego is an internal defence mechanism that Rama developed to self assess and introspect about any complaints or opposition he gets from the world. It is typical of Rama's worldly interactions, that when someone meets him for the first time, they are usually meeting him in his status of Respect and Success, as perceived by them. And the next time they meet him, they would feel like they have surpassed Rama in status and no longer feel the need to show Respect.

Rama has neither fallen nor has he risen in status, respect or success. Where he is, is why there will be balance for all. This is a response to those who have come after Rama, but "grew" beyond Rama as he is not perceived as unmoving. Rama, without trying, was setting a standard. Let's say the design speed of a road was set up to be 100 Kmph. When you go beyond the design speed doesn't mean you will surely crash, it means that you are risking your life. Standards have a purpose.

Rama has an extensive social network and therefore is quite perceptive of his image. He carefully crafts it with honesty and without deception. He believes in his Motherland's motto, "Satyameva Jayate".

Rama says that words must be used sparingly and only when required. Words carry power. So, when one exaggerates their role and says that it's difficult to raise children and that they are not sleeping until 1 am. The child who is usually asleep by 12 AM is indeed up that day until quarter past 1 AM. As if the universe is listening and letting you know not to exaggerate things. Not everything needs to be spoken. Not every stimulus warrants a response. When you speak limitedly, you only need to speak the truth.

CHAPTER 19

TIMELY MARRIAGES

Are a key

Timely marriages are a key to unlocking some of Life's most important secrets. But how does one know what's the correct time for marriage? Rama had studied the age of marriage in the generations past and present, in order to properly assess it.

When we are in our pre-occupied states of mind, we only smile when the photographer asks us to smile. It's hard enough to figure out a right time to smile, knowing the right time for marriage is practically out of reach, if we don't pause, sit down and self assess.

In the context of all the various thoughts going on in Rama's mind, such as the 7 lives, re-incarnation, progressing of souls through the 7 stages to Salvation, one of the most important stages in each of these lives is Marriage.

Marriage brings Families together, marriage grows families, so families may continue to come together and grow further. In simpler times before Rama arrived at the "Philosophy of Family", he was of the impression that the "Purpose of Life is Life", in that, Life exists to continue on, in that, people live so they may bring new people to life.

These new people must be wanted, cared for and nurtured so they are able to continue the tradition of life into the future. We, the present forms of life are not the owners of our lives, we are its grateful resident custodians. Along with this custodial duty, another additional duty on us is to progress on the path of Soul Maturity.

Life is a chance to attain the maturity of soul toward purity so pure, it qualifies to rejoin the Paramatma. And because this purification of the soul is happening on Earth, the additional requirement of having a zero karmic balance must also be met.

Soul Maturity progress, is yet another feature that is available to impart, but doesn't transfer automatically to the offspring. It has to occur in the physical world via oral teachings or practical applications. The receiving soul attains this progress upon successful practical application and inculcation.

Therefore, the Soul Maturity Progress of the parent-to-be may not have so much bearing on the time of marriage. The maturity can also be physically imparted and maybe done throughout the coexisting lifetime of both souls. This process can be visualised with the help of Relay track events with small modifications.

In this Life Relay Track event, the run doesn't end with handing over the stick, though there may be an actual handover of worldly responsibilities. There is also a ceremonial handover which stands for the imparting of Soul Maturity. This Relay event will continue on for the duration of their lifetimes and both the runners continue to run. So, when there are 4 generations of people living in the same family, all of them are running, imparting to each other each other's soul maturity.

The other factor that needs to be considered in assessing the right time for marriage, is the physical well being of the bride and the groom. Rama is all too familiar with the problems of late marriages. He sees those around him suffering the consequences of not getting married at the right time. Physically, the right time to marry is when you are the healthiest. That is when all the bodily functions both physically and emotionally are in their best form.

Considering how this event can be easily qualified as being very close to the purpose of life, it is bound to get complicated, convoluted, twisted and turned. But then again, if it isn't challenging, it's probably not worth playing. Competing interests and sometimes unaddressed pettiness, can make this process of Marriage quite a difficult one.

There are factors such as previous karmic balance that influence the birth family and circumstances of the groom, qualities of the bride and her family and vice versa. The event of Marriage is only just the beginning of a lifelong alliance. The sacred alliance that forms the very foundation of the society we all live in.

Marriage must be supported by family. Raising children must be supported by family. A wholesome upbringing of a child lays a solid foundation for the child's growth into a happier and harmonious adulthood.

But, when this doesn't happen and children are left to the mercy of the circumstances that the world throws at them, the gaps that are created will be sure to enter the fray when deciding not just that particular person's future but that of his present and future family members. Some families can take a longtime to recover from these gaps.

It doesn't take a lot of physical strength for an adult to slap a little boy, in order to discipline him. It takes more than strength, it takes bravery and courage, to discipline yourself to never raise a hand on a helpless child, regardless of your reason, to never physically or emotionally abuse those weaker than yourself.

To use the sacred institution of marriage to enforce your hegemony over your own family members, or those of your in-laws is also an abuse of your position of power.

Let's say somehow you got lucky and you had a timely marriage, what life secrets are you unlocking? The first, quite obvious secret that's unlocked is, how powerless you are when faced with the real challenges. To face these challenges, it's best if you are fully equipped with all of your physical and mental faculties.

Marriage is the event that you will be unofficially pushed out from under your parents protection, and pulled up for becoming their protector. There will be a learning curve which requires a lot of physical energies and mental faculties, so don't wait until you are all used up in making a salary.

The second secret that's unlocked is that, had you delayed your marriage anymore than it already had, you'd be crying blood tears. Because your body, in trying to hold the family together, is barely standing.

Rama's intention isn't to paint a dire straits image, but to face up to the fact that most of the marriages occurring are late marriages. Parents are using up their children as ATM cards as long as they possibly can, and not really taking interest in getting their sons and daughters married in time. On the other end, Employers are squeezing out every drop of creativity from these unmarried minds.

Also worth mentioning are the social and real world pressures, of high cost of living and skyrocketing costs of child care. Those who should be getting married are scared to even think about it. People are rarely considering marriage before 30 and by the time they are through with the hunt and settling down with a partner, they are hitting 40.

At this age, it's a miracle to have one child. Dedicated parents realise that it's in the best interest of their child to have a sibling and follow through with it, but not all children are lucky.

The lack of timely marriages is an unofficial one-child policy. Lack of timely marriages, is in effect a drastic population reduction plan of action in motion. Lack of timely marriages is the root cause of so many social ills, it's mind boggling.

As Rama is on the topic of Marriage, he wanted to spend some time on an item on its periphery. One of the reasons behind reluctance towards marriage is a pre-existing affection to someone else. The "L" word gets thrown into the mix when it's really the "Life" in its desperation to find the best match. Someone with compensating attributes, on the journey to Soul maturity and eventually to Moksha. With all its years-long and many times lives-long training, the soul seeks out another soul that completes it. Which is probably why the field of Physics proves opposite poles attract. In the attraction of souls, one soul brings with it what the other soul lacks. It is yet another example of the Inseparability of the Spirit and Matter, where the behaviour of the matter is exhibited just as curiously in the behaviour of the spirit.

Marriage is the coming together of souls for the purpose of birthing new souls into the world. In this Clash of attributes, the best of both worlds emerge victorious. The attributes with lower intensity will lose to the attributes with higher intensity. It's not the quality or the virtuosity of the attribute, that is at play, but, the Soul's innate commitment, passion and power to fight for that attribute, that is at play. There is no faking in this fighting, it's all internal. Which is why it's not just enough to teach kids the right values. It's equally important to teach kids how to fight for those values. It can literally make the difference between their Salvation and Damnation.

Returning to the "one that got away" obstacle in the way of timely marriages. It's not even a real problem, because there is not just one chance given for the souls to come together. It's at least 7 multiplied with the number of all offspring and offspring of offspring produced in the journey. The coming together of souls that got away from each other, in the form of offspring is more likely to happen than it's not. Having bigger families is going to improve those odds. Matches missed now will be matched later, so there is no point sulking about it. The soul that's coming together in this life, could have very well been the one that got away in the past life. Think about that and cheer up!

CHAPTER 20
ROLE OF A TREE

is to give shade without asking questions

One of the lines, from an inspiring book that captured Rama's attention, was about how one plays a central role, but not knowing it. It was once again the application of the same old cliches, to make us feel good, but can be interpreted to mean anything one wants it to. Like the daily horoscopes section in newspapers, where everyone has a wonderful day.

A tree can't really choose not to give shade. One can't escape their nature. Like when someone might immaturely suggest that it is destiny that drives our lives, but in fact, it's our very nature that drives our lives. This isn't a fight between people, but a battle between natures that were forged into being, over a long time. Our nature, the code in our DNA, not just the appearance, but the behaviour, the responses, the principles, the unseen, and the barely understood life force that makes us who we are.

It's the person's Kartavyam to stay true to his nature. Believe it or not, by definition, nature is already written. You may try to add to it, but modification of nature typically occurs in offspring, as a hybrid of 2 natures.

Modifications to nature are a lifelong exercise with imposition of heavy tolls. One example is that of Genetic punishment.

One aspect that can be ascribed as being the gold standard of the life of our planet is the suffering. There is so much suffering, most of which is inflicted on people by other people. People punish each other for not being kind to each other. Sometimes, it seems to Rama, that the Universe or Nature punishes the offspring or their offspring for the crimes committed by predecessors. Almost as if, attempting to remove any remaining traits of punishable behaviour. Rama, being gentle and kind hearted, felt sympathetic to the suffering, but also acknowledges that the journey, to join back the Paramatma, wasn't going to be an easy one.

Holding the son responsible for his father's debt is a way of genetic purification, an organic defect correction and an adaptation mechanism for the changing circumstances. Unfortunately, there are societies where this practice still occurs as a crude and harsh way of changing one's nature. In the modern times of no accountability, this is, at least ostentatiously, frowned upon, but the practice nevertheless goes on.

Another example to explain the phenomenon, is to take the same set of circumstances faced by 2 different generations, but only one of them is successful, while the other suffers. The successful generation is a direct descendant of the suffering generation. The suffering generations are the carriers of the circumstances, whose duty it is to survive. The descendants, the inheritors of the same set of circumstances, will succeed when the time arrives.

It sometimes needs a different time to become successful. Until such time the same thing shall be done over and over again, and when the time comes the same circumstances are actually the ones required to deliver different results. It's almost like hiding the secrets in plain sight, until the moment they are actually required, at which time the secrets reveal themselves. This part may be destiny, which Rama won't discount or dispute.

Which is precisely why it's critical that we understand our nature. For example, Rama learned that his anger doesn't last long. Understandably, his compassion lasts longer than his anger. Rama thought, "If I didn't understand this feature of my nature, I would be burning bridges all day long only to go back and build them back with great difficulty".

The better one understands their nature, the easier it will become to play their role. Nature of a person is strongly tied to the nature of his family, just how you can only always get mangoes from a mango tree. To maintain the Integrity of this family tree is not a choice, it is part of the Purpose of Life.

CHAPTER 21
TIME TRAVEL

was always possible

Rama had a curious mind. To take on the most challenging questions of his Time was important to him. One such question was whether Time Travel was possible? He proposes that Time, like Space, is a constant. To travel in Space, you travel physically from a point on the Fabric of Space to another point. In travelling through the Fabric of Time, you may not do so physically. It must be done within the mind, from one moment on the Fabric of Time to another moment. Time travel is the journey from one decision making moment to another. In Rama's vision of Time travel, the purpose for Time travel of a person must be more important than the actual action.

The purpose for time travel preceding in importance, to the person's effort to create time travel apparatus and eventually venture on their journey through time, does not seem unreasonable to Rama. A person, armed with his purpose, travelling through time becomes more potent than any apparatus that would be used to travel through time or even the journey itself. You travel in time with the purpose of undoing a past outcome or to create a new one. When the purpose is achieved, it means Time travel was successful.

Time Travel has to have a purpose. Everything has a purpose or a reason for it. The air blows because of the difference in pressure and temperature, the river flows because of gravity, the birds fly for food and everything else that is, it is because of the reason or a purpose behind it. Without a purpose, any work would become pointless and the purpose has to be personal. Because, your entire world only exists because of you. When you're done, so is your world, but you're almost never done, as you will have found another way to exist, perhaps in a different time and form.

Rama's past encounter with a theory of Time travel was when a friend presented a reasonable explanation to him. It was more than 10 years ago, when he suggested that it's we who move through time and that the time stays constant. Rama moved to debunk it immediately by suggesting that while moving through time, you don't stay constant, i.e., you grow older. Therefore, when your ability to do things changes, it means something changed and the ominous tick-tick-tick sound that was heard, in the meanwhile, was none other than that of time. The response from his friend was silence, as Rama secretly revelled in his spontaneous burst of wisdom.

Rama went on... "Only now I realise that I should have taken this up at the same time and thought deeper. Instead of responding without fully thinking it through, I should have listened further and then responded. I wish I had used the opportunity to arrive in the current present thought 10 years ago. Now that I'm doing this, I'm indeed travelling through time by making the decision to explore time travel. And, until such a moment I choose to make the decision to stop delving into this specific topic of time travel, I'll reside within it. I will have access and ability to all other decisions, with an option to make the next decision at any time. As this particular aspect of my Time Travel is ongoing, all other aspects of my existence will continue in their own timelines. Which means that "i" already exists in several timelines, through the means of various aspects of my life that come together to define my complete existence".

i - the imaginary number in complex mathematics, in Rama's view corresponds to each person, and the wave functions explained by this "i" are his life's journey.

In attempting to extend his train of thought, Rama was amazed where he was going with it. Time exists within the Person dimension and his decisions (derived from his reasons & purposes connected to one or several or all aspects of his life) are the special vectors that allow the person to move forward or backward in the motion dimension.

Another way to visualise this situation is, where time is moving through the person dimension where his decisions are the vectors that are causing him to switch from one timeline to another. Here, imagine several timelines flowing through this person dimension, causing many timelines at various stages, corresponding to various aspects of that person, to flow through the person. Person's daily routine keeps changing based on his decisions.

Returning to the visualisation, where a person is the vector in one timeline. This is a much less complicated visual than visualising all the timelines flowing at the same time. His decisions are scalars with magnitudes ranging between 0 and 1. Here, when a change in decision happens, the person shifts to the next timeline with an entirely different set of axes, defined by the scope of that decision. He stays in that timeline until another decision is made.

During his time within the timeline, he has access to all the time of all people, when other decisions may be made, and therefore has existed and will continue to exist, in all of them. It's important to understand that the time will exist, but the people themselves may or may not be still in the same time. They are most likely to have made other decisions and moved on to different times.

We're all indeed on perpetual time travel, moving from one decision to another. Time being the medium of travel, enables our decision making. Decision making is the most defining aspect of being a human being. Therefore, by extension, unable to decide is surely going to be a reflection of how existent we really are?!

In Rama's view, Time, contrary to popular understanding, is a constant and only we the people keep changing.

Another principle that Rama proposes in support of his Time Travel theory, that's seldom fully comprehended is that, "anything that can be done can also be undone". Exceptions to this rule are 3 events. They are Life, Death and Gravity.

The object travelling isn't the body, but the mind. This addresses the concerns of ageing, thereby debunking Rama's own earlier debunking, there is no age for the mind as the mind isn't the Brain, but the Consciousness. Going a step further, we can consider that the genetic material is flowing through time through procreation. In this process the mind becomes replicated and fully refreshed through birth, and the time travel continues to continue continuously.

Going back to travel through time.

What's the trigger? How do we go about travelling through time?

If decisions are triggering a jump in dimensions, then by that definition our action of becoming aware of said knowledge and making an appropriate decision will also constitute a time jump or travel. An opposite decision will mean a jump in the other direction. The path sometimes could be circular, which means there are no forwards and backwards in this time travel. Sure there are clockwise and anticlockwise, but if the road goes both ways, any direction you choose will be the right path. By extension, any path that is circular is bound to be the correct one. A real world example: A circular economy is a sustainable economy is the correct economy.

Another Example: A decision to get a certain type of education will allow you to shift to a travel path that you would not have otherwise travelled.

The topic is best explained and understood with examples, so let's go through a few more...

Let's say you visit a tribal reservation and you become aware of a way to brush your teeth with tender neem branches. After this trip, you have made a decision to brush your teeth with tender neem branches only, and no longer use toothbrush and toothpaste. In making that decision, a time travel has occurred and away you went. Some might say ahead and others backwards in time, but since Time is a constant, we're simply travelling through time with the trigger of our decisions.

There may be any number of timelines that we may be going through at a given point. For instance, as for the timeline relating to the subject of brushing your teeth you have moved through time while all other timelines pertaining to other aspects of your life may not have been affected. Similarly, with relation to another aspect of your day or your routine or even relating to your life, any change or decision that happens in you, with or without interaction with others will constitute a time travel. It's not important to acknowledge whether we're moving ahead or backwards on a number line. It's more important to fully appreciate the fact that we can indeed move from one point to another by simply deciding to do so; the movement graph is more likely something close to a circle, with points on its circumference, of all the possibilities of things that can occur.

Time can be visualised and understood as a natural sequence of events like a number line. -1 comes before 0 and +1 comes after 0 and then comes 2, then 3 and 4.

To put it in simple terms... Time travel to the past or the future is indeed possible in the present through interactions with people, whom you perceive as being from different times.

In interacting with people from ahead of your time, in the sequence of events, you will have been made aware of their present, your potential future. In making a conscious decision to follow them into their time, you will have travelled to the future.

Similarly, in interacting with people from behind you in time, you will have been made aware of their present and your potential past, you may or may not be aware. In making a conscious decision to follow them into their time, you will have travelled to the past.

It's also possible to travel through time without any outside interactions. Because the mind can, within its power of imagination i.e., in interactions with the self, visualise a change or a decision through the process of thought. Upon a conscious decision to make a change in one or more aspects of your life, you will have achieved time travel.

Arriving at the question of why? Why will someone be motivated to travel through time, be it either forward or backward on a natural sequence of events? What is the point of time travel and what do these interactions, that can trigger decision changes in one's life, mean?

Rama's mind has thought about this sufficiently enough on its own to dream up a differential equation to show how the Equation of Life works. Integral of t from birth till death, doe x squared by doe x equals X. x is the person dimension through which the travel was occurring and not through time as Time is a constant. X denotes the state of transformation achieved in the person's lifetime. The person is travelling through time, by consciously travelling within his mind to that decision making moment in Time. He is Time Travelling for the purpose of making a different decision and thereby changing things.

All the good and bad that ever existed can be done away with a conscious decision to undo it, by travelling back to that decision making moment. As is evident from daily news, time travel occurs with everything. An extreme example of time travel would be that of the creation of a Nation, with the adaptation of the Constitution. Any person who can travel to that moment and tear up the Constitution, causes the nation to become undone. In order to protect a nation, all necessary steps must be taken to prevent people from altering the circumstances of the formation of a Nation.

Every decision you are making is enabling the travel through time and the lack of decision making prevents it. In certain things that have achieved a state of stability and harmony, no additional decisions will help. And in things that need improvement, additional decision making is needed.

As Rama documents his theory he feels like he's channelling a theoretical physicist. And, in dreaming up the differential equation in the person dimension, he feels like he's channelling a mathematician. Such discoveries in the depths of our minds make the food a bit tastier and make our lives a little richer, as we experience our own existence a bit more closely ".

Rama thanked himself for taking the time to explore time and travel in it. At this point he is consciously deciding to time travel back to his regular timeline.

In the general context of things, such as 7 lives, reincarnation, soul maturity and the latest thought of Rama on Time travel with a purpose, it helps to understand that the conscious decision making is driven by the consciousness, which is an attribute of the soul. In other words, the Soul drives the mind to travel from and to, decision making moments.

Rama realises that there can be so much work that can be added to the concept of Time travel, but at this decision making moment he is consciously deciding to pause the time on the aspect of Time Travel. He is choosing to time travel to the moment before the Time travel thought had occurred.

Time travelling and the Pursuit of Truth are both travelling, one in the pursuit of another. One travels through time and finds the Truth. And in the Pursuit of Truth one finds Time travel. One fundamental understanding that's worth a memory burn is this... no matter how far one drifts away, they are never too far away from the Truth. Truth is the wormhole in the fabric of Time, that has the ability to connect moments that are otherwise light years away, within the time it takes for the person to reach it.

CHAPTER 22

THEORY OF CONVEYANCE

Content, Intent & Compassion

Rama is living his life in an ordinary manner, but his ordinary life somehow has a running commentary. He may just be going to a shop, the commentary just starts off narrating every single detail… What is this, why is that and how should it have been? Even Rama thinks that this is funny. Things don't have to be so detail oriented and serious. He is the first to wake up and the last to bed in his household. To say he is incharge of his life would be an understatement.

Rama travels back to a moment of his past, which means his mind would be focused on that previous moment of time and therefore won't be able to capture his regular timeline's developments in extreme detail.

In yet another new job, Rama took in a distant land, he came across a local who engaged him in an important conversation regarding the various modes of communication that were in use at the time. He was having this discussion with a few people from work while they were on their way to lunch.

Rama recollects that afternoon quite fondly. He and some co-workers were walking over to a nearby restaurant. On the way, he was telling them about a recent observation, "I find it very fascinating that even though we attempt to the best of our communicative abilities, it is very common that people interpret it in a way that is very possibly different from what we are trying to convey". One of the co-workers responded, "Oh, I know; like email, I've sent out emails that have been misunderstood before". Which raises quite a red flag about email, as this tool is used for most of the official communication all over the world.

He went into further discussion about how our brain just interprets any information supplied to it in a unique way. And, this information is stored in the memory, forever in the way it was interpreted. In a way it is, for all internal and resulting consequences, the individual's reality. Now consider the very same process applied to each one of us, where there may be all these versions of reality that we cannot even comprehend. A very simple example to understand what Rama is saying would be, when 2 people are given the same book to read. By the end of them finishing reading, they will have taken away different things from it. That is their Reality of what the book was about, and it is how it will be remembered by that person forever.

While Rama is still talking, one of the co-worker says, "You know, Rama, I can see you having discussions on university campuses", he responded with "thanks". He was pleased with his thoughts. They went back to work.

On that weekend, he drove to the closest City to connect with friends. While at dinner, he was telling a friend about his newly found observation. By this time the process had reached a state of how inefficient and un-evolved our communication process has been thus far. The discussion that ensued was even more profound than before. It was in the lines of, what we should be looking for in order to better convey the exact message to the listener? "The content of the communication, even though very important, combined with the intent or the reason for the communication, improves the quality of communication", is what he said to his friend, who was pleasantly impressed.

With the inception of the idea, he was thinking about how far his and his friend's realities could be. No wonder people have so many issues communicating with others. Also, it was noted that people, including himself, were deliberately conveying just the content of the message. In retrospect, it sounded quite silly. Ever since then, Rama went on to apply this idea to all serious communications he was involved in. Whenever he noticed that the speaker was not providing the intent of the message he is attempting to convey, he subtly went about enquiring the background instead of just assuming it.

Another couple of weeks later, on a drive back to another city he discussed the same concept with another friend of his to further his understanding. It was an hour long discussion, over which he asserted his views on the concept and better articulated the theory for his own understanding. Whilst the conversation, there was a conscious effort from both sides to communicate with intent intact with the content, in every aspect of the discussion. It was a fascinating experience for Rama, when the concept he had just introduced was already being applied by the person who was listening.

The concept is on the right path, it proved itself. It was able to succeed in making the listener respond in perfect harmony and with no confusion, like it was interpreted exactly how the speaker was trying to convey. By additionally introducing compassion for each other into the mix, people can have the most meaningful conversations.

The Theory of Conveyance, as devised by Rama, states that the conveyance factor is directly proportional to the combination of content, intent and the compassion within the conversation. The quality of the content, the transparency of the intent and the general compassion exhibited toward one another will determine how much of the message is conveyed across from the speaker to the listener.

Prior to the practical application of the theory, each was right as per their own reasons and wrong as per the reasons of others. This wonderful perpetual magic of both sides stating exact opposite things being both right will continue until both apply collective effort to rectify it. Otherwise, it's probably the feature of quantum mechanics where multiple states of the particle are said to exist at the same time and no one will ever understand why.

If you want to, fix it by applying the Theory of Conveyance and having a meaningful conversation, else go on with your life. Remember, that if something stood hanging long enough, without any resolution, it doesn't matter that much anyway.

CHAPTER 23
TRANSFORMATION

of all things into Money

The physical and chemical transformations are covered in the Law of Conservation of Nature, that goes something like this, nothing is created, nothing is destroyed and that it only transforms from one form to another. These laws of science have got it slightly wrong.

They used to be correct at some point, but now they are not. The Laws of conservation must be renamed with something more appropriate. Here's an idea, "the Law of Transformation of everything into money" and the law must state, "there is nothing to conserve, because everything is already used up and what little is left is also earmarked to be used up".

It was Rama's favourite pastime to observe. The obvious transformation of things to money was understandable until it also affected the things of sentimental value. Things with sentimental value just meant that they would go for a much higher price. Even sentiment has transformed itself into money. Where does the stooping lower stop?!

The modern definition of a developed world means that we have arrived at the singularity, that absolutely everything is or can become money. Which of course brings us to the most eerily ominous sound, resounding in the eardrums, "money is everything".

The abolishment of slavery also seems like a ploy, because modern day slaves were required to be given a semblance of freedom as part of their sustenance. This was required for the safety of the slave owners. As the then modern times rolled by, the slaves started figuring things out and taking things into their own hands. Quite similar to the current modern times, when the modern day slaves are figuring things out and how, most likely, it's not going to end well.

Rama is quite the perfection personified type of personality. He acknowledges that it is not his duty to solve other people's problems himself, but with the help of the medium use all his work to show how people may be able to solve their problems themselves. Which is the main reason behind the elaborate concepts with explanations forming themselves into a rebuttal to the books. Books that promise freedom, but end up making the reader more vulnerable to the evermore sophisticated traps of the contemporary world.

He has no ego, he doesn't jump to judge people, he holds no grudges and is not easily distracted. But, there is one thing that bothers him. The indentured servitude of all animal life including humans as being the bedrock principle of human civilisation. Not even an 8 year old can be convinced to believe that the wonders of the world were built by the workers upon their own volition, in pursuant of their freedom to choose the nature of their livelihood.

The easiest way to achieve mass compliance, is to monopolise the currency and artificially increase the needs of people to infinity, so the barter economy is no longer practically feasible. Which means, every human interaction would then be sanctioned and sanctified by the use of official currency.

The parallels that can be drawn between money and the transformation of lead into gold are dangerously close. Of course the transformation into Gold was presented as purification of the soul with some spirituality thrown in, to keep the hope alive. After all, hopes, aspirations and ambitions of unsuspecting people are what are keeping the world spinning. Rama hopes it doesn't come to where it one day becomes okay to say, "I'm enslaving you for your own good", or maybe the day already came and went and Rama simply isn't ready to accept it.

If you are not already enslaved by those closest to you, you are surely to be targeted by someone else. The voluntary trafficking of adult children to other countries by their own parents is by far the worst development one could have hoped for. To make it so that you hate everything about your home country, that once you leave you will never return, at least not until it's too late. The aggressive use of reverse psychology is how it's made to be believed that someone else's self serving propaganda was not just your idea, but your life's soul purpose.

This happens because there is a narrative that cannot be questioned. The narrative could very well be called, "How to not achieve your dreams and be completely satisfied about its acceptance". The sheep in human form for all their talk are all baa-baa-blinded when it comes to knowing what it means to do right by your children.

The chain of doing right by your children is a sacred one and one that ought not to be broken.

What does one really dream to be? After removing all the ideas that were implanted into your brain as an unsuspecting young child, by self serving do-gooding imposters, you will be left with maybe a few dreams of your own.

Unless you want to be beaten over your head to wake you up from your dreams, figuratively speaking, you better fall in line and forget all about your dreams, is what 99.9999% of the people will tell you. 99.9999% of the people will tell you this because that is what they are doing and they are driven to propagate the message, but, why? For the lack of a simpler way to put it, it's because misery loves company. Perhaps more importantly, the majority are miserable and those who are miserable hate those who are truly happy.

Rama feels like this thought is going round and round without coming to the point. It is not a complicated point to understand, but it is the hardest to implement in one's life. Which is why it seems, his mind is not yet keen on allowing access to the main point.

If all things transformed into only one thing, and that one thing is Money, people also just become like money. As a result, instead of people becoming useful, they become useless. The way the employment parameters are stacked, the more potential you have to build things and solve problems, the harder you will be kept away from the service of humanity. Which explains why the best of the best minds are targeted for employment and paid handsomely to work against the interests of mankind.

The only people who are truly free, it seems, are the true intellectuals and the idiots, while everyone in between is busy being enslaved. The voluntary nature of this enslavement should never be lost on anyone who can sense the crux of the point attempting to be made here, because that is where the solution exists.

If people are volunteering their lives away for money, money is where both the problem and the solution must exist within.

Chapter 24
MONEY

became the Language of the World

One of the most famous lines and by far the most inspiring to Rama was when an inspiring author suggests the language of the world. At the time of reading the book, Rama was still quite young and was impressionable to romantic ideas laced in flowery words.

This particular revelation that Rama is about to make, did not come as a surprise to anyone but himself. It was the realisation that Money is the language of the world and it was a major disappointment for Rama to finally come to accept that it was.

What's even worse was that not only did it become the only permissible official language of the world, but it went so far as to replace the soul of the world, the Paramatma. An infamous Hindi line goes like this, "paisa mein Paramatma hai", i.e., "In Money lies the Soul of the World".

What this means is that the devil himself is masquerading as God. Money, a mechanism to trade with ease, is per se not the devil, but everything other than the tradability of it, is. The way it is created, distributed and leveraged is the biggest problem. One might say the same for gold or gold-backed paper as currency, because some countries have more gold reserves than others. Yet another unfortunate fact is that the countries with the most people may not have the most gold reserves. How could such a set of circumstances possibly be fair?

It's not perfect, but at least it's not paper. The age-old demand for Gold might be drawing from human nature to like shiny things, but the demand for paper is quite literally silly. And maybe that's why there isn't that a real connection and therefore nobody saves it anymore. Anyone can pick up a piece of paper and print numbers, pictures and words on it and it would not be that much different from what's considered money, except for the forced acceptance of only some papers. It's all Maya, the whole production is fake yet somehow the emotion it generates is genuine. It means real emotions can be created from fake inputs, just like a movie. Scriptures called it the theatre of the world, Jagannatakam.

Rama, with all such superficial thoughts flowing in his mind, realised that he had not connected with the Wise-Soul-within, in a while, but that is to be expected. He recognises that to expect the Wise Soul within to comment on man-made problems with no meaningful depth whatsoever, is beneath him.

Rama was taking stock of things and where they are... we have Money as the Language of the World. Most people would say that it should be Love, as in "Love is the Language of the World", but Love is a meaningless term outside of its context. Rama would say, "Compassion is the Language of the World", but as is evident it is not.

While every other culture in the world are proud of their ancient cultures and are committed to protecting and preserving their sacred heritage, our country stands reluctantly. Sanskrit should be the National Language, but it's not. The mediums of preserving a language are the literature and art forms such as music and movies, have no interest in doing so, as is evident in usage of Hindi words in Bollywood movies - there are barely any. At best they serve as conjunctions, which is not nothing, but it's very close to it.

Rama strongly believes that this downfall of the civilisation and the ethos of the society is directly correlated to Money becoming the language of the World. People have been conditioned to a compulsory relinquishment of the custodial responsibility to their residing culture in order to get ahead.

What chance does a Mother tongue have when mother's themselves take pride in discounting the culturally rich native languages?! People will stop at nothing for a loaf of bread, metaphorically speaking. Money will make you do anything if that means you'll be fed your next meal. Money in this form is akin to the devil himself.

CHAPTER 25
MOMENTS

of Truth

Rama thinks, "The reason I choose simplicity and skip complexity in things, is not because I can, but because I can't handle any more complexity than I already do. It is not a privilege that I'm choosing to exercise, but a moral obligation for the sake of my physical and mental well being. There is a major difference between the two, and in addition to that there shall continue to be major gaps in people's perception, (at times even my own, if and when I'm careless), of what's happening and why I'm doing something.

Others want to attribute the worst, instead of affording you the benefit of doubt. Doing so allows them to keep their own insecurities at bay. My well being is the first priority, not how people perceive me. Because things are fragile and if I'm not careful, it'll all be for waste and another life awaits. I mean no offence to life, but, I'm done. Therefore, this particular decision is not really a choice I'm making, but me being duty bound to my destiny".

Rama recalls an episode from his journeys abroad, where he explored the world of Art for an extended period of time. Rama lives in his mind more than he does in the real world. Even on his journey with Art, the experience was quite similar. You can't expect a sportsman to also take care of fixing broken appliances at home, because his dedication would be to the sport. Rama's focus was on Art.

While pursuing Art, Rama hadn't realised that the world had moved on to newer inventions. The most basic tools that had become widely prevalent were missed by him. There is always a price to pay, and his long journey through the Art world was well worth it, thought Rama, never once doubting it.

The world of art and the power of expression that it brought with it, had finally opened his mind to the next level. From there he could take decisive action, not just stand on the sidelines, while the world that he loved so much was being handled so badly.

There were so many revelations that the Art world had so generously showered upon him. As he was thinking, he recalls one of them. "How we treat our young ones and how we treat our elders. The difference between the two or the lack thereof, tells you all you need to know about the kind of society we live in". Rama would like to think that regardless of the kind of society we are living in the present, it must aspire to do right by its citizens.

What can one person do? The obvious answer is to lead by example.

We have a lot more control over our lives than it is made out to be, and for infinite reasons we are kept from ever finding this out. But that's not to say that we control our destiny. We don't. There is nothing to control. Destiny is the exact opposite of control. It is the achievement of zero karmic balance by the way of purification of the soul, in order to attain Moksha and join back the Paramatma.

Another moment of truth was the mainstreamed phenomenon, of deliberate extension of the duration of waste. First, you will be forced to "learn" for as long as possible. And, when the bulb comes on, it'll take as long as it'll take to unlearn all the junk. Everyone knows that some things they do might be a waste. But, the moment you realise that the trap has been set, not just for a few things but for the whole thing, you cry as your efforts go to waste, whilst your opponents increase their odds.

It almost feels like this game is maybe being played in an opposite manner. Instead of you striving to get ahead, you are fighting tooth and nail to push your competition back. The competition will sabotage, lie, cheat and do whatever it takes to waste as much of your life as possible, as they stay focussed on the target. What do they know that you don't? Could there be a limit to how many people can get Moksha in a day?

If you fall for this trap, it'll be considered nobody's fault but your own. There is no court or tribunal set up to deal with such petty grievances. It's a high stakes game. You can only bet your life and gain Moksha or you come back for another life if you lose. You come back for another life, until you win Moksha.

Being young and excited about the things you discovered along the way is the most natural response. Not all may share the same excitement. Your excitement in sharing the same with your friends, may not always go as planned. Rama was out on a hiking trip with his friends. He had just realised that the "material things don't mean anything" and to prove his point he took a ring from his friend's hand and threw it away. Within no time he realised a quantum shift in the emotions of his friend. He underestimated how much material things can mean to others.

Rama went on to search and find the ring with great effort. He regretted his action. It was unnecessary for him to prove whatever he may have learnt to others. He learned this lesson the hard way.

Something may mean nothing to you but for a whole lot of people it can mean a lot. Even if you are not lying to yourself and others when you say, it's all maya, and it means nothing, it does not. It's all Maya, but it means a whole lot to everyone. If it didn't, people would be resigning from their jobs like there was no tomorrow. They wouldn't even be taking the jobs in the first place. Even now, there are a lot more people looking for jobs than there are jobs available. You must get it through your head that material things mean a lot, and there is nothing you should do about it.

Understand very carefully that your enlightenment was meant for you and you alone. To share with others, must be done in such a way, that it's just the right amount.

It's the toughest job!

Meditation teachers are also doing the same. They are doing the toughest job of providing the right amount of knowledge, not more, not less. They are not buying ads, or selling services. You are pulled to them because there is a calling and you sense the belonging.

Chapter 26
NATURAL

State of Lying

Lying comes to humans as naturally as breathing. To expect from humans to be truthful, is to ask them to go against their natural instincts, internal urges and every fibre of their being. What is also a natural state is all the hoping and praying for all others to fail. Rama's natural state of not lying and wanting all others to succeed, indeed seems unnatural. It is therefore bound to be met with fierce resistance.

Lying, cheating, scheming and manipulating are natural survival and defence mechanisms. Asking folks not to lie, not to cheat, not to scheme and not manipulate is simply foolish, prima-facie. What also came naturally to Rama was the next obvious thought to rationalise such behaviour. He says that even though most people may lie, cheat, scheme and manipulate, the world keeps on spinning for those who don't. All others are just riding their coattails.

"But, no, this time I'm going to stop short of rationalising", thought Rama. "Why? Why must I try to make sense of it all? Will the world not go round if I don't make sense of it, of course not, why then continue the futile effort. Whether or not things make sense to me, the world spins on and people go about their lives, and so must I", thought Rama.

Rama recalls teaching subjects to a fellow student, who couldn't follow the instructions of the teacher nor of the world. Student succeeds and the teacher takes credit. What came as a surprise was that the student gave credit to the teacher and didn't mention Rama. Student doesn't want to give credit to Rama, but why give credit to the Teacher? Because it's good for optics. Rama was picking up the slack when the teacher wasn't doing his part. But, why is the teacher taking the credit? Teacher knows that Rama helped the student and also that he didn't help Rama. Rama figured such things out the hard way. It was difficult to learn the subject, but he didn't hesitate a moment to share the lessons with others. But, why did the student not want to credit Rama? In acknowledging the help of a peer, he would make his success your success, and when you are seen as successful, his success is not that valuable.

Rama was not perturbed by this development at all. Each has their own Karma account book, they are accountable to.

Each is given a minimum of seven lives to go over the curve and attain Moksha. Inability to achieve the state in 7 lives will mean more lives. Could a lack of awareness or a deliberate mismanagement be the cause of the huge backlog in Moksha attainments. And, in a round-about way, the root cause of population related problems?

Academic Education is a sure way for a good life, no one should ever doubt that. But, not all should continue to continue on that path forever. Because, at some point, when you are satisfied, there is a responsibility to leave the opportunity for a good life to other people. Using academic education to continuously get ahead may not be a great way of life. Getting ahead by getting more education sounds fine but will you ever use this education?

If you can wrap your head around it, you will realise that a "rich spoiled brat with an excellent taste in things", does more service to the society than by becoming a disciplined employee. There is wisdom in saying that those who have enough, must not work more to make more for themselves. After all, accumulation and distribution is how the world goes around.

CHAPTER 27

TOUGHEST JOB

Is Doing the Exact Amount Needed

It is easy to do more or less than required. Doing less creates problems and so does doing more. Doing less is perhaps less tough and doing more is most likely to be more tough, but it is the hardest to do the exact amount of work that is required.

The smart one who has figured things out, will do the minimum amount of work that keeps him from getting fired. The not so smart ones who haven't figured things out, will do the maximum amount of work they can get done, also to keep themselves from getting fired. Those who do the exact amount of work required, are the ones sure to get fired. Not because they were wrong, but because they threaten the status quo of having an ill-equipped workforce.

The blame game that ensues over non resolution of decades old problems, cannot be allowed to continue. Especially, when there are those who can in fact deliver the exact amount of work needed to solve the problems.

Then, there are those who think they can save the world. These are usually the knuckleheads that weren't properly trained, but have watched too many great movies, who got carried away in their passion for service unto others.

In a world of liars and opportunists, the one who sets out to save the people on the strength of their word alone will be the one who needs saving. He surely won't be able to save anyone. The thought of someone choosing to save the people, might suggest that it is them who might need help the most, has crossed Rama's mind. In any case there must be a strict criterion, for how one qualifies for your time. Mistakes happen, but if you have the right attitude, the self scrutiny you put in place should prevent the mistakes from happening. Rama would like to believe that he is taking the toughest jobs and only doing the exact amount of work needed.

What is the exact amount? It is the amount that solves the problem completely and if possible forever, but doesn't leave any excuses for others to slack off because of it. In the guise of solution provisioning, if you try to solve all the potential future problems you are laying the foundation for problem-ridden future generations.

Like writing up a document with principles, rules and procedures and asking people to follow the document. This document ends up in the custody of a few and the rest are kept as far away from it as possible. Why would people follow anything? Even trying to enforce with fear only works for a short period of time. If only things were that easy!

A one-size-fits-all is the definition of a go-to solution and it occurs because tailor made solutions, although the best way forward, are impossible for the makers to achieve.

It's easy to assume that someone who is older in age is a better individual. Like expecting more manners from someone who is older in age. This is not an absolute truth, yet it happens all the time. Genuine manners, maturity, decency and courtesy are a result of fine parenting and family values. Attributing such virtues to age alone is an insult to all the commitment, hard work and resolve that goes into moulding an individual into a decent human being.

It's easy to pawn off your duties onto someone else and hope things get done right. But, to expect protection from outsiders that one doesn't get from one's own parent, is an insult to the child's natural intelligence and is a downright child abuse on part of the parent. In the instance of raising children, doing the exact amount is also doing the maximum amount that there's to be done. Doing less is a sure ticket for another life for the parent and maybe even the child.

CHAPTER 28
MIDDLE CLASS

Must become an Inspiring Movement

The Term "Middle class" has taken on a negative meaning to itself. These are the ones who do what's necessary, without shying away from doing what's required of them. They also never go overboard and do or show off more than what's required. These are also the ones who are actually, truly and genuinely aspiring for a minimal impact, socially and environmentally conscious life.

Only consuming what's required - is the lifestyle that probably has the best chance of surviving the longest if not perpetually. Why and how can that be a negative thing?

Middle class can't just become a statistic that boxes people inside or outside of it. It's a mental state where you understand and attain a delicate balance with your surroundings. A mental state that works hard everyday to review the things that are allowed, need to be allowed and are no longer allowed.

Doing all that is required and only that, is the principle that has the discipline and accountability built into it.

Middle class living is what must be aspired to, so our children and their children for all times to come can continue to be a cradle of life and all the possibilities that it brings. Middle class movement expands the state of mind to not exploit and pillage, but to balance. It is a voluntarily achieved delicate balance with Nature, not to plunder the planet but also not suffer while maintaining self restraint.

How is this possible when no one wants to live an ordinary life? There is no such thing as an aspiring ordinary human, at least not yet discovered. People are unique except for their natural needs. People are exceptional in their own ways, but in humility and to each other they are sadharan manushya, an ordinary human. An ordinary human with a middle class mentality is one who will alter the course of humanity for all time.

Rama had a middle class upbringing and he appreciated all the care he received while growing up. Considering the burden of his birth circumstances his immediate family members bore, some might say he fared okay. It's not that hard to fathom, that if you never let a child walk, he will become disabled not because he was born with the disability, but because he was never allowed to walk.

The role of parents in shaping the children cannot be overstated. Middle class or not, to fare okay, even after being subject to the harshness and cruelties of an ordinary life, is not a small task. It also speaks volumes of the society, when a vast majority of the lot seem to be having decent lives.

CHAPTER 29

ONUS UPON US

To Know Ourselves

Rama recalls the thought from his exploration of Circle Of Circumstance and other concepts, that Moksha is the Purpose of Life. Moksha is the goal and knowing yourself is the key.

In efforts to know himself, Rama occasionally runs a sounding board exercise to see if he can learn about himself. This requires input from others. All his peers are happily living their sophisticated lives. They generally talk less and seldom talk to him. It takes two to tango, and if one is not dancing, it's most likely that they can't dance. If someone has not connected with you in a while, it could mean that they have nothing to say, or more precisely nothing to say to you. The path to self discovery is hampered when you can't connect with others. An important question to ask oneself on the path of knowing yourself is, are you better when you are along with others or are you getting better, at their expense?

If you are better, when you are with others, that's okay, if you are better, when you are by yourself, that's also okay, but if you are getting better at the expense of those with you, that's not okay. Onus upon you isn't just to pursue your destiny, but also constantly verifying whether your being the way you are is beneficial (or even neutral) to the collective, or is it actually hurting the rest of us all, as you thrive and prosper. The former is okay, but the latter is not.

It's quite possible that you may be at the receiving end of this very phenomenon. Knowing others can help avoid potential harm and also be useful in knowing yourself.

Yet another way of viewing things is whether you are first to blame the person before considering his circumstances, because they do end up determining the majority of people's behaviour. People lie, all the time. These are circumstances dictating the way of life. Lying is part of survival mechanism for those who can't make ends meet on their honesty alone. You may lie to the whole world and it won't matter much because they are probably lying to you too. The lies that matter the most are the ones you tell yourself. It is akin to the highest form of betrayal. In doing so you are committing the crime of high treason.

How much can you really know about yourself on your journey to self discovery, if you keep lying to yourself? When you muddy the waters, whatever you do find out, could just be a version of a lie you told yourself in a weak moment. It takes courage and strength to venture inward to know yourself. It'll be ugly, even shameful at times, but the reward is going to be perhaps the most important lesson of your entire life.

What is Truth? As general as the question may sound and as varied and broad the answer to that might seem, the closest to the True Truth is you knowing your True self. You may know all the Truths there are to know in the world, but if you don't find out about yourself, the truths you learn may just be ticking time bombs, waiting to blow up in your face and in the faces of others.

It's like a thief, who doesn't know he is a thief, but knows the secrets of his country. When the moment comes the thief will sell out. That is the problem with not knowing oneself. Had he known he was a thief, he would probably wake up from the illusion he's living in and steer clear of all important things he's a part of and limit himself to stealing things that don't matter. Because he may be a thief, but he can never imagine being a traitor to his Country. This is the easiest test. Go ask any crook and he would acknowledge that he would never betray his country for selfish reasons. He might even deflect the blame saying he is doing what he is doing, because he thinks what he does doesn't matter. This journey of self discovery is not just for the virtuous and the righteous, but is equally important for everyone else.

It is the Kartavyam of every Individual to find out about his true Nature and be True to it.

CHAPTER 30

GOD

Is Not Petty

Rama acknowledges that all paths in all the books he read, are indeed about discovering and thereby achieving one's destiny. He is in no way discounting the contribution of the books to the betterment of the society. In fact those books have inspired this book in the most fundamental of ways. This book is however a response in the negative. It's not that the books misunderstood the man or his destiny or even his journey toward it, in fact Rama endorses that they got all of that right.

They understood the man correctly and therefore were able to win the hearts of so many men and women from all walks of life all around the World.

Unfortunately, it needs to be said that they got God wrong. God isn't so weak and petty that he would only be able to help you at the last moment. Coming to your rescue just before you forego your destiny, and that too if you were lucky enough to have chosen it in the first place. God is all pervasive, omnipresent and therefore, omni-available to all, that he never leaves your side. He is inside and constantly helping and guiding; bringing you back when you may get lost and cheering you on when you keep doing the right thing.

When a book gets a man wrong, it may be excusable as long as the damage done is repairable. But when a book gets a God wrong, it misses the main point and therefore is totally fair game to go big guns blazing, even at those that may themselves be big guns.

CHAPTER 31

FIRE INSIDE

Is the driving force

Fire that's burning inside us is the force that is driving us. This Fire is what paves the path by melting the obstacles away. The Fire makes us do things, break barriers, go the furthest places and achieve incredible tasks. We know what it makes us do, but do we know why it is inside of us? What is it that's inside of us that feeds this fire?

The desire, that's born in the soul of the universe. Rama hasn't thought about it in this way before but as he did, he realised for the first time that the phrase "the soul of the Universe" and the "Paramatma" mean the same exact thing.

The desire and the Fire may not be that different either. The soul desires, among other things, not to burn in hell. As Rama was taking the liberty to expand the train of thoughts, he thought that perhaps the fire inside could be the fear of hell.

Among the many contested theories of the world, only a few concepts remain broadly accepted by almost all ways of life. One is the great flood. Another is that there are 3 worlds, one is where we live, one beneath, also known as the hell and the one above, popularly referred to as the heaven. The 3 worlds are stacked on top of each other.

Rama suggests that when the weight of the living world increases, the burden on it becomes more and more, it goes closer and closer to hell and thereby farther from heaven. The burden isn't the number of people, it's the weight of the sins they carry.

Like the credit card debt that pulls you closer into the traps of the loan sharks and farther away from Financial Freedom. The burden isn't the number of the people, it's the amount of debt they carry. The overall burden is going to be averaged out to the individual just like the National debt. Generally speaking, "we the people", make the world either hellish or heavenly for each other.

Hell and Heaven are on the same planet. The dimension in which these worlds are accessed is the person dimension. The ascendance to heaven is akin to the successful completion of the 7 lives with no karmic balance and the soul rejoices as it rejoins the Paramatma.

The Fire Inside is our super power to escape Hell and ascend to Heaven. In the context of the 7 lives, the intensity of the fire inside to escape hell would probably be highest in the earlier lives. In the later lives the fire inside is more like a simmered down flame. Associating the fire with the desire to be successful in life, may tell the story about how the most fearful among us are those who are strongly driven to build things and succeed at life. Those who are the bravest and the most courageous, have practically no desire to prove to anyone else that they are, or can be, successful. This interpretation essentially turns Success on its head and changes its very definition.

As he is going through all these levels of exploring the Fire Inside, Rama feels the uneasiness about the interconnectedness of all concepts with each other. Why can't they all just be where they are and exist separately? It can get really challenging, convoluted and complicated to traverse the landscape when there is so much rocky and hilly terrain to cross. Each concept is a challenge in its own right.

The Wise-soul-within who hasn't chimed in in a while wanted to take part in some action and comment on his Roommate, the Fire Inside. He said to Rama that these concepts do exist separately and are only getting connected in the person dimension, as and when the person is connecting these concepts.

Here, it is you who are connecting these concepts, because they are connected to you. Otherwise the concepts are simply existing quite independently and separately in the minds of the people and the books that captured them. These concepts may be connected by one person and coexist in him or in multiple persons and coexist in their interconnectedness. An example would be the actions and thoughts about marriage and children can coexist together in both the wife and the husband.

That was a bit profound, thought Rama. It got touchy feely there for a moment. Maybe because he was rambling on about his warmth providing roommate, the fire inside.

The Fire Inside is also what keeps us in check, Rama thought as he uttered to himself, "my tastes are too rich to skimp on principle" and this is possible because the Fire makes sure of it.

CHAPTER 32

PERSONAL SOVEREIGNTY

Must be Respected

It is quite common in the constitutions of all great nations to grant the freedom of movement as being a fundamental right to its citizens.

Respecting a person's personal sovereignty and his constitutionally protected right to freedom of movement become closely connected, once you accept that there are destinations one reaches beyond the height, length, width and time dimensions. Rama is referring to the Destinations in the fifth dimension, the person dimension. Movement in this dimension can only be possible when personal sovereignty over his domain remains undisturbed.

A person's right to pursue his Life, without any undue influence of others is what constitutes the preservation of a person's personal sovereignty. An outsider attempting to influence another to further his own self interests, must be considered a violation of that person's fundamental right and be punished accordingly. All countries that defend and fight for their own national sovereignty may do so, by first empowering its citizens with personal sovereignty.

If there is a covert campaign or even a public campaign to influence impressionable minds and brainwash them to think a certain way; where a balanced approach to thinking and decision making, in order to enforce accountability on the part of both sides, is not allowed; Or if there is any activity that aims at distracting a person from relinquishing his personal sovereignty under any pretext. Such acts shall be deemed as an act of war on the sovereignty of the person and shall be dealt with utmost severity.

Parents and close family members are the first line of defence against such an incursion into sovereign spaces of children. Protection and preservation of the Personal sovereignty of children is a sacred duty. A society that can understand, respect and thereafter take measures to ensure a policy based framework in this regard will have a solid foundation for not only its citizens, but for the society as a whole. A society which holds sacred the personal sovereignty of its citizens, will have no trouble finding stakeholders to enlist themselves in the fight for National sovereignty. Personal sovereignty helps with striking the right balance between our personal lives and our social lives, i.e., where to go further and where to stop.

One of the values taught to us as children is to help others. Isn't that the most virtuous thing to teach children? Rama thinks that it is. But that's also what it is, a value for the children. As adults, we are expected to traverse complex facets of life. For example, the practical reality is that when you volunteer as an adult to help someone out of the goodness of your heart, you get a push back. People, rightfully so, get suspicious of your intentions. Contrary to popular belief this is not their ego, that's preventing you from helping them, but is a function of personal sovereignty.

Personal sovereignty becomes the guiding principle in a person's journey to Moksha. If the National sovereignty can only be preserved by the way of protection from a foreign nation, such sovereignty is only limited to the paper it was written on. On the same lines, if I need you to attain my Moksha, can it be attained?! Rama doesn't think that Life is a school test where a teacher or a fellow student can help you get through it. In attaining your Moksha, you are the teacher, you are the pupil, you are the benefactor and you are the beneficiary.

CHAPTER 33

I

can't lie

As Rama emerges from the Personal sovereignty and the utmost significance of respecting it, he stumbles on to one of the most defining aspects of his own Personal Sovereignty, that he wishes to be respected by others. It is that Rama can't lie. It's an inability to bring himself to lie. Sure he lies, everyone lies, about things that don't matter in the least, but he can't lie when it comes to the things that truly matter.

He can't lie, because he decided not to come back for another life. Because, Truth is Salvation and Salvation is the Truth. In telling the truth you find yourself. In lying and pretending, you only find myriad different things that the lies you speak make you into, creating distortions distracting you from the destination. The only thing you ever need to find is yourself. Not gold, not anything else, just yourself. Who are you and what is it that you value? Finding yourself is the key and the rest will follow.

How many keys are there, how many can there be, thought Rama. There must be a few.

Has this thought crossed Rama's mind before? Sure, it has, or maybe it hasn't in this particular form. Is Rama repeating himself to himself? There is bound to be repetition. Important things will be reminded over and over until they are always remembered. You internalise something so strongly that it no longer needs reminding, that's when the repetition will stop.

Your mother will keep reminding you she is your mother, not in so many words, but from all her actions. What happens when you go far away from her and you are no longer reminded of her? You will forget that she is your mother. You may not forget her literally, but you will forget all about all the care she has given to you. That is the natural principle of "out of sight - out of mind", at work. Since you've forgotten all she should have meant to you, your obligation of reciprocation back unto her is also forgotten.

The Mother, as powerful as she was bestowed, can only be that power through her children. This development reflects back to her, that she allowed her children to get lost in the fray, and it is for this shortcoming that she bears the brunt of becoming oblivious to her own children. The same exact thing applies to the Fathers. When you don't care for your children properly, including inculcating the values that are required for stable living conditions, that's on you and there shall be correction. Hitting where it hurts the most is Nature's way of correcting the wrongs.

What transpires in the outside world and what is being embarked on the inside, may have no correlation whatsoever. Someone may be imprisoned for some action but, inside this entrapment may be the path to his enlightenment waiting to reveal itself. The path, however unconventional, shall always lead forward on the journey to re-meet the maker.

If someone knew what they were doing was wrong they may not do it, but if they do, that's wrong. If the same someone is trapped in such a way that he can never know what's right, that's wrong too.

This has 2 angles. 1, obviously they don't know that they are doing wrong - so their actions are out of ignorance, and 2, the truth about their actions has been deliberately kept secret from them, so they keep performing their assigned duties without any questions. People are kept in the dark for so many reasons. People are all there are in the world, some of them are hurting and some doing the hurting. We, the people, are the be-all and end-all. We are the seller, we are the buyer and we are the product.

Each physical and mental suffering is an opportunity for advancement, but rarely is suffering considered a good thing. It's not forgiveness that's expected and neither can we change the course with punishment. In punishing people for every small wrong, a bad example is being set. Over-indulgence of the outside can mean that the inside world is getting less attention than is required for a proper balance.

Penal codes have been in place for a longtime and are still failing to deter people from committing crimes. In defining the crimes so precisely, the Law is inadvertently becoming the tool of choice to exploit the loop holes, game the system and get away with it. In addition to the understanding of the bigger game that is at play, to show the right path and to help as much as you can, is the only thing that can be tried.

For all this to transpire in the most beneficial way to all mankind, the pursuit of Truth must go on undeterred. Life is nothing, if it's not deep. How exactly does this fair with Rama's long trusted philosophy of, "if it's not simple, you maybe doing something wrong" ?

On one hand there is nothing simple about understanding the depths of our most basic daily routines, and on the other, Rama won't proceed further on things unless they are clarified and simplified beforehand. The ensuing clash of the concepts, where complexity and simplicity must coexist within the mind of the same man, determines the kind of life he experiences.

Maybe it's part of the job to simplify things and organise well. These are the What and How of Life? What is it? It is a complex structure. How is it possible to cross it? It must be done so with simplicity.

Lying complicates while telling the Truth simplifies.

It might seem counterintuitive because lying seems to simplify a lot of things on a day to day basis. It does not. You are becoming stuck in the quagmire, that'll keep you trapped in it. When you try speaking the Truth, you'll quickly realise that at the moment there may be some awkwardness and inconveniences, but the next interactions with the same people will be cake walks. Because, they won't bother with you, nor will they bother you anymore. Suddenly you are free from the burden of lies that were sure to follow, had you chosen to lie.

Unfortunately, it is difficult to express in words the joy of freedom from the burden of lies. It is best experienced by one's own journey up the path of truthful self discovery.

Chapter 34
WORLD

is not a cake walk

The world isn't here to be some kind of a cake walk, we were entitled to, it's here for its own reasons, as are we. It's a tough place to be. Most perish simply because and for no known reason. Life is wasted on things so insignificant that its meaning becomes clearer, in its end than its beginning and middle.

A child grows up with all he has learnt, and then as a grown up he learns that all the learning other than mathematics and languages were unnecessary. All the dreams built in our mind, were just distractions from seeing and learning the real reality. The best you can hope for, is preventing the lie from repeating itself again.

There is truly no greater treasure to be found out there in the world, that you cannot find within yourself. The world outside is only a reflection of you. What you beam out, beams back at you. Practically speaking, what you beam out, was already in you, so why take the long route.

There are hunters and there are the hunted and then there are those who are done with all the games in their past lives and are ready to attain Salvation. The third kind are the most dangerous as they have the most to lose. A world filled with people, without any identifier about the kind of people they are, cannot be a cake walk.

In the story of the hunter, hunted and the hunt, one must be at the top of their game to hunt when they are hungry. To hide when being hunted. And most importantly, roar like a lion and inspire others, as they're getting ready to leave behind hunting for the goal of Moksha.

CHAPTER 35
DREAM OF A TEAR

in the Fabric of Time

Rama sometimes grows fatigued, as the inside world keeps taking a lion's share of Rama's waking time. And, when he goes to sleep, the inside world has him in his entirety. In one such dream was an exciting little episode of the popularly understood kind of time travel.

Rama was able to jump from one place to another, as if there was a tear in the fabric of Space. The time it would take otherwise to travel between the places just vanished into thin air. Rama was disappearing from one place and appearing in another, like shown in the movies.

There were several other dreams that he had that were quite vivid. It is well understood that whatever you keep thinking throughout the day, is what you may end up dreaming about. If someone has entered your dreams, that means they have entered your mind to a deeper level. This person may not be forgotten that easily.

But, Rama wasn't thinking about what happened in the dreams. He's thinking about why and how this much sophistication was possible inside his head. He did nothing extraordinary to achieve this ability. Children as young as 1 year old can have vivid dreams.

How different are dreams, really, from imagination, visualisation and instant actualisation of thoughts? On a day when Rama made a life changing decision, as he was to embark on the ship that took him on his journey to the distant land, he had the most profound life experience. As he sat on the floor waiting for the ship to sail off into the ocean, he found something in his bag. It was a food parcel that his family had packed for him, despite him insisting not to do so. The parcel reminded him of the affection he was missing in the distant land. He wasn't particularly hungry but seeing as waiting to become hungry was only going to make the food go cold and stale, he decided to eat.

As he put a spoonful of the food into his mouth, no later than a fraction of a second later, tears started rolling out of his eyes. Rama had so many incredible life experiences, but this particular moment tops them all. This moment set his entire future in motion. Until this moment, Rama had no intentions and ambitions about what he should do next. After that moment and by the time he completed the little food parcel, he had planned out the next big move... the permanent move to return home to his family.

Things were never the same after that moment at the port town. After that, each waking moment was spent on planning and preparing for an exit from the distant land. This was not going to be easy, because it would be akin to swimming against the tide. No one would understand an exit, just when he was about to enter his prime.

Can dreams, really, be as impactful as imagination, visualisation and instant actualisation? Sure they can be. Rama can attest to it from personal experience of having had the, "you should do new things every day" dream. But because dreams tend to be forgotten, their impact can fade instantly.

Another well known understanding is that there exists a parallel universe for every possibility, thus suggesting infinite parallel universes. Rama's take on this understanding is that the number of parallel universes is not infinite, i.e., not every possibility gets a universe. It's only those possibilities the mind wants to explore, with commitment, gets one each. Parallel universes are not just there by default, they have to be launched, sustained and maintained.

Also these universes are not literal. Just because you wanted one, that there would not be a new big bang that eventually results in your desired possibility, no. Here the word Universe can be interchangeable with the word World. These are more like angles or various aspects within the same life. If you are an artist, that's a world. If you want to have an engineering job, that's another world, and everyone has a world for their family, another for their friends.

One may have about 10 worlds, someone just 1, and the others any number, but it is definitely finite. Not because, theoretically it can't be infinite, but because our brain capacity to juggle through all these worlds is, practically speaking, finite.

CHAPTER 36
TAKE A SEAT

there is a lot to cover

One day Rama was invited to speak at an event. Rama addresses the gathering, "Popular belief that Life is a series of choices is an utter lie. It is a duty. Those who taught us to pursue wealth and treasures couldn't be more wrong. It's not about the pursuit of wealth, it's about the preservation of Treasure. The world is our Treasure".

Someone from the crowd stands up and says, easy for you to say, you are flush with cash. Rama responded, "be that as it may, what is it that's preventing you from preserving the world that is our treasure ? ", after hearing Rama's response, the man took his seat.

The education system, the institution of family and a philosophy of transparency, are a few ideas that can be brought up for discussion at this point.

The meaning of life and the purpose of life may sound like they are the same thing, but they are not. Meaning is what it means to you in the moment, what it meant in the past and what it will mean to you in the future. This is your perception. While the Purpose of life is the perception of you and what you mean to the world.

When a young mind is being trained, so he may grow up to face the world confidently, the education provided to him becomes the toolkit he brings with him everywhere he goes. When this toolkit misses important things, the child becomes open to attacks with not enough defences.

One of the key lessons missing in this toolkit is the one on the most basic impulse of Jealousy. We are taught about greed, dishonesty and to an extent about jealousy, but only as an extension of some other element. To the obvious dismay of those who care, we end up becoming greedy, dishonest and the exact opposite of all other such virtues taught to us. Rama attributes this behaviour to a misunderstanding of the inherent element of Jealousy.

Jealousy is the main reason behind a lot of animosity between people. It's not right to ask people to stop being jealous and perform the act of disingenuous virtue signalling in one form or another. If jealousy can be prevented by asking, there would be a lot more happiness in the society. It's much more effective to not show off your successes and excesses, in order to prevent people from producing a feeling of jealousy against you.

There must be caution exercised when opening ourselves to proselytism. An idea must qualify as a success without a hint of doubt before it can be promoted to others. You can't just promote an idea because you have money or power or some book of tricks in your hand. It can happen in an open, free and a transparent manner. In an open, free and a transparent (OFT) society, Stupidity with a mask of popularity can never parade in the streets as Intellect or Power. An OFT Society is an ideal society, but it is only possible with the help of a wholesome education, caring families and a transparent policy.

The society that is not desperate will not take shortcuts, in the pursuit of glory. It won't fall prey to trickery in dreams of easy money. And it certainly doesn't trample on the lives of some, for the sake of some others.

Teachings such as "one must laugh a little, just not at anyone's expense" and that "they must live a little, just not on another's back" will usher in an era of harmony among peoples. What must be happening in our country, should not just be the building of roads and buildings but the building of minds. For far too long, the minds of our countrymen lay dormant for one reason or another. The economic exercise is poised to create roads for the cultural revolution, which will once again usher in the new dawn of individual liberties and the renaissance of an authentic Bharatiya life experience, that was once a beacon of hope for mankind. Bharat will once again become the standard-bearer of an aspirational society the world so desperately needs.

Rama thinks that for this to happen, one must become immune to the words, be it in praise, in insult or in proselytism. It's not easy!

CHAPTER 37
MAN MONEY

is born from the Respect it's given

Respecting money like the Respect given to people led to money becoming like the mighty man, a.k.a Man Money; and man becoming mere money, i.e., only respected for their net-worths and used as mere tools in transactions. No one listens to money per se, but they listen to the person controlling the money. That's why in our current form of democracy, there can be no true democracy, there can be only oligarchy, i.e., where people's destinies are dictated by those with money.

Man becoming money might sound like a negative development, it doesn't have to be. In whichever role the man is playing, that results in his value increasing cannot be a negative development. On the face of it, if it takes a lot more money or energy to summon a man, that's his value. It's to be noted that it's not always a good thing that the value of a man is too high. A Doctor's or a Lawyer's value cannot be too high, because then it'll mean the value of life goes down and the price of justice goes up. Both of those are negative developments.

The main difference between the Money Man and the Man money, is that the Man Money doesn't have a choice, but the Money Man has it. Money

Man can choose what he wants to have for lunch, while the Man Money for all its respect doesn't have any desires of its own, but is driven by the desires of its controllers.

Rama who is a strong believer that Life isn't a choice but a duty, can be seen here talking about Money Man having a choice. There is no need to be strict sticklers to all the words, with an on-point commitment. Rama only spoke about lunch and that too in the context of Money. If things are always serious, Life being the duty it is, can feel like a drag and become quite boring very quickly. Where's the fun, if we are always complaining about things.

The precise moment, when money becomes Man money, is when it can exercise its choice on Man, even if it's another Man making the call. When there is at least 1 degree of separation between the person making the call and the person affected by the call, it's the Man Money that's in play and is playing the man. Rama calls this Money the Choice Rupee (Rupee with a choice), the turning of Rupee into a Man of action.

Rama acknowledges the fact that the comparison of Money to Man feels demeaning to Mankind, but he also recognises his role of being the bearer of the message and not the cause of the demeaning action. Within this context, which is quite a serious one, the entirety of humanity is being subjected to the whims and fantasies of those who control the Money. If there was really a choice afforded to people all would choose to end it. The lack of choice is the opportunity for real work. The fight between Man and Man Money is one destined for the history books. Because, it's really the fight between the Man and the Man skulking in the shadows. Not because he's waiting for a fair chance to fight you in the open, but because he's waiting for the right moment to stab you in the back and take you for all you've got.

The thumb rule here is that you can't do what you want to when someone is paying you a salary. It's called a full time job for a reason. In other words, when you want to do something you want, you cannot be on anyone's payroll. When the world is set up so you get paid for being some place, know this, you are not going to receive any payment when you are where you want to be. Most of us can't get past this obstacle, because there is no such thing as free food.

CHAPTER 38

THE BIGGEST TRAVESTY

is how much Truth is kept from people

The probability theory would suggest that at least 50 percent of the Truth is kept from the people. But Rama has a hunch that this number is about 99 percent. For all the red carpets, supposedly laid out for the education of people, hardly any wisdom gets through to the pupils.

The biggest travesty that was ever perpetrated on the family unit, was the premise that the independence of the individual was paramount to his success. The second biggest is, how our natural storytelling ability was limited to only a handful of people and groups who control every waking thought in our minds. A family member gets a job and suddenly he is the Master of the Manor, the Lord of the Castle, the King of the Palace. So shallow is the depth of the ocean of education, a toddler can crawl through it unharmed. Yet, somehow have adults, drunk on power, drowning in it.

The third biggest travesty of life is, its presentation to its subject as a choice when it's indeed his duty. Traversing life as a series of choices, taking shortcuts, finding escape ways, dereliction of duties, etc., will all attract punishments. Not always directly to the subject, but in their harshest forms, such as the punishments and suffering imposed on their parents and offspring. Giving examples here, Rama thought, might account to cruelty on his part and therefore moves on.

The purpose of the wise souls isn't to give solutions, but to teach you how to find solutions on your own. Much like the proverb about teaching a man to fish, rather than giving him one. One such lesson was the story from a wise man called the Pencil story.

There lived a father and a son in a village. The son was a student in the local village school. The son loses his pencil and eraser almost every day. Son was not concerned about this fact as he was just a kid. He doesn't yet realise that he may be taken advantage of, on a daily basis. Father notices this but he also doesn't make a deal out of it. He simply gives his son a new pencil and eraser when necessary.

The father had complained about something else to the management the previous year and it became a big deal. Father had also complained about another thing earlier in that academic year, and it wasn't well received. Father accepts and appreciates the stand of the teacher as he was not necessarily all knowing and therefore can take a hint and knows when to shut up.

This was why the Father has decided not to complain about the lost pencils and erasers. But was this the right thing to do?

Well, if he complains, he's adding to the burden and pressure the teachers are already under. Since the financial loss was not a big one for the father, he was choosing to prioritise and make sure the son gets the best from his teacher.

But what about the lost pencils and erasers? If the son was throwing those away himself as some game, that is something, but since it's not being made into a big deal, it'll eventually stop.

What if it's someone else, who may be regularly taking his son's pencils and erasers? What if it's another student? A young student who is casually taking other students' belongings. Are there other students, who are also missing their belongings? Was the father's non complaining attitude, encouraging negative behaviour in that student? But, if he did complain there was also the added complexity of back firing and drama, which the father was not willing to risk.

There are 3 potential things that can happen. 1, The father complains and becomes the bad guy. But, he ends up inadvertently helping the student by stopping the bad behaviour early. 2, The father doesn't complain for reasons previously mentioned. 3, Then there is the bystander, who takes the side of the non complaining father. Why should the father complain, when those stealing are weeding themselves out of the real competition?!

The wise soul says to Rama, there will be several stories such as this one. Each of us will be part of and all the various angles of viewing the story. When a story gets told, it's usually the view of the observer that gets written. Just as Rama was telling his version of the stories he has read in the books, his story too,will be retold in many different angles. The fundamental right of an individual to express covers the right to his own interpretation of the works and words he encounters along the path.

Most don't even know that such a right exists, much less exercise it. This right to interpret is how accountability comes back into play. Creators of works have to be mindful of how things might be interpreted and therefore do a good job in telling their story. The right to interpret is also how the individual is freed from the clutches of the media mafia that wants to control every thought in people's minds.

Oftentimes, the story that is being told may not be finished. Much like a series, with a prequel and a sequel, not necessarily in order. A listener of a story, a hundred years after the fact could very well be the one to make it his own, and start a new chapter to the story or be the one to finish it.

The next time someone is telling you a story, you must not only assess the story, but also assess the person telling it to you and their circumstances. The mind won't be applied to things before simply transmitting it forward to others. Like repeating a news story in the guise of making small talk, without fully considering whether they are furthering a propaganda or a genuine public interest. If you are not mindful of such pitfalls, you end up becoming your own personal travesty.

CHAPTER 39

LAST LIFE

Philosophy

If God has written everything already, your destiny is also already written, isn't it? No. Rama considers the role of God to be that of a videogame designer. He created the game. He'll show what the end would and could be, but, it's up to the player to win the game.

When you fail at a level, you don't go to the next level. You have to play the same level until you win, for you to enter the next level. Therefore, 7 lives aren't necessarily the same as 7 births or 7 deaths, they are 7 levels for you to finish the game. Unless you learn from your mistakes, and apply them to overcome the obstacles, it's quite possible you may be stuck in the level loop for a while.

In the last level, the player is bound to be extremely careful, attentive and maintain strict discipline. No compromising on principles, no shortcuts and no cheat codes, because he might be able to sense what's at stake. Therefore, he won't take any chances at risking the successful completion of the game.

Finishing the game isn't about pleasing anyone and showing off, in fact no one will ever know. It's only to please, and to prove to, oneself. Hence, with the attainment of Salvation, one achieves the final respite from the cycle of life.

Rama is all for working on everything himself and trying to do as much for himself, himself. Because this, he believes, is indeed his last life and wouldn't return back for another Life. He's consciously working on getting all the karmic balance completed in the best way he can, by himself.

Fortunately, it is not required to be done all by yourself. We all need help and could use the help of our family and friends on this journey of journeys.

It is easy to say and write, but achieving it is another story. As Rama truly believes that this Life is his last life, it'll take all the work it needs for him to get across the finish line. All the information regarding how much exact work it will need is not available to Rama. What he can do is not neglect the obvious pitfalls. One of which is the negligence of the family. Family is the source of ultimate strength of an individual and the neglect of the same could spell disaster. One angle for consideration is the possibility that parents may not always be a higher life number than their children. Which means that they may not fully appreciate their offspring's journey to Moksha. It's because they are not ready for it just yet. How to address this major gap between family members?

The feeling of gratitude between each other for having each other needs to be in place, before any meaningful help can flow between souls. To be grateful to one another is the prerequisite to understand each other. This could be done easily by extending the benefit of doubt by telling yourself, "you may be able to understand your parents when you yourself become a parent".

What might parents want for themselves? Generally speaking, they can't wait for the kids to grow up because they want to, once again, have their pre-children lives back. Freedom to do whatever they want without worrying every moment.

Next question, is how much each other's expectations affect the real relationship? Sure, the children didn't ask the parents to give birth to them, but how long will this be used as an excuse for the unrelenting onslaught of responsibility after responsibility. And, of course the inevitable angle, where the children grow up and want their lives back, from before their parents became old and needed care.

As is evident from the changing landscapes of the family homes, all these responsibilities are becoming too much to handle, causing people to quit their families. Quitting jobs seems less likely to happen than quitting families.

Why is this happening now? Or was it always like this? The protection and preservation of the Family was perhaps not supposed to be easy at all. Wouldn't this be a perfect criterion for screening people and keeping them out of some special club? Fully acknowledging the possibility of being dead wrong on this, Rama proposes a scenario where conditions are conducive for Moksha.

The son must be in the father's house, because the father cannot be in the son's house. In order to do that, they must all be together in the same house that is inherited. The son can repair the house or make a new construction there, but he cannot ask the parents to come to another place; even if asked they will not come happily.

Living like it's your last life with the attitude of clearing the karmic balance, is a philosophy that'll push people in the right direction whenever they are facing a moral dilemma.

Whether it is Rama's last life or not, the experiences that await him must be endured everyday, by finding ways to be at peace with himself and with the world. In a world that has no distractions, finding peace may not be a problem. But in a world that's filled to the brim with nothing but distractions, finding a moment of peace can be the hardest thing. No matter how small the duration of peace you seek, it can happen with effort.

Rama's friend who comes from a farming family has shared with him a personal experience. Rama who is a son of a chartered accountant was excited to learn about a story from a farm. For the past few years his family were into sheep farming. Apparently, all those years when there were sheep at his family farm, there was no peace at home. Members of the family were always at each other's throats. The house felt like it was a living hell. Recently, his family has fallen into some tough times and they had to sell off all the sheep. Using some money they bought a few cows for sustenance. No sooner had the cows settled in at the farm, a palpable sense of peace and calm has set in.

Rama's friend had once heard from his great uncle, upon asking for a business idea, that one must not be in the business of alcohol and meat because it involves suffering of souls. As this story was being shared, the wise soul within Rama said, "You will never harm a soul when you realise that that soul is no different from your own". Rama felt as if the wise-soul-within was channelling a spiritual guru. Rama in response to it said, "you will never harm a soul, not even your own, nor will you allow any harm come upon your soul from others".

Rama's friend acknowledged that there could be other reasons why his family started experiencing Peace and calm. But, in reducing the negative karmic balance, by moving away from the meat business and into the milk business, he sure felt lighter.

The Karmic balance, it seems to Rama, apart from determining the progress of your journey to Moksha, also dictates your day-to-day suffering and peace of mind regimen. "If peace of mind is what you are looking for, don't harm a soul, how hard can it be", thought Rama.

Rama is reminded of all the inspiring books along the way, where the main character in the book is physically going to places and sharing his experiences. In doing so, the author brings his readers a world travelling experience. In his own work, Rama is not going to physical places, but is only recollecting his memories. In all the various depths he is exploring, he's providing a deep dive into the mind, an another worldly experience. His readers can take it with them, even if they are not going anywhere.

His inspiring authors, the Masters, had sent their characters to places. Rama had stayed put in his seat, as he took his audiences to the never explored corners of their own minds.

CHAPTER 40

DEBUNKING

the protagonist

A typical protagonist in the inspiring books was always playing the numbers game. The bigger the group of family, friends and followers the higher the chances of success. The thing that's the most true about being friends, is about having some business with them. Simply put, one has friends because they are in business and one has no friends because they have no business to offer.

Desert Nations sell dates so they may buy rice. There isn't a bigger truth than this in World commerce. This trade creates friendship. Thus far is a well established fact. Here's the kicker. Just because someone learned why he has a lot of friends or doesn't, doesn't mean he's going to break from his own character, flip his life upside down and change things in the friends department.

Rama thinks to himself, everyday he's not being a sheep, trying to be like someone else, he's winning. A protagonist in a book always wanted to be a shepherd while Rama, on the other hand, never once wanted to be a sheep. An interesting observation about the oldest lie ever told and the greatest lie ever sold, is that the latter used the former as an excuse to capture people's imagination.

Rama likes to think that he's a Realist. A Realist always debunks a Theorist. A Realist is a person who understands, respects and lives in the actual physical realities of his life and doesn't fool around with the fantasies of the mind. Maybe that's the problem, Rama thought. Nobody lives in reality anymore and that's why real problems are not getting solved. Everybody is busy solving imaginary problems, so they can feel self important, while contributing nothing meaningful to the real world problems.

Protesting in the streets about climate crises half-way across the World while his family's and his community's state of affairs are left unattended. This is because of the fear of exposing our truly shallow commitments to things that matter the most.

A Theorist has to lie everyday in order to keep his job. He compromises on his principles each hour. He hates himself every waking minute of his life. He is his last line of defence. How do you expect someone to defend someone whom he hates? He won't. While the theorist is busy busting himself, a realist is doing the same while also exploring options to free himself.

One is said to be bonafide free, when he has the freedom to not lie. Real freedom allows a person to appreciate themself. Which is precisely the reason why being free is of the paramount importance, in order to live a truly fulfilling life.

Rama pondered a bit about the works that had inspired him. The titles of books, he thought, would have been more appropriately named in the lines of, "How to not achieve your dreams and be completely satisfied about it?". For those readers who don't like long titles, one word titles such as, "Acceptance" or "Distraction" would be fitting.

What good is literature, if it's only used as a pass time or some kind of entertainment? Literature, as self respecting creators will attest, is created to inspire. A Realist, must as his duty, debunk the theorist by respectfully annihilating the lies sold to people, in the form of books filled with half knowledge.

There is nothing wrong with being of limited knowledge, as we are all works in progress. However, the disclaimer about the limitation of one's knowledge, must be displayed in big and bold font on the earliest page possible.

CHAPTER 41

BIRTH

Of Energy

A new life is born as an expansion of the energy fields, of two existing lives. The Heartbeat is the rhythm of all the particles within the energy field, oscillating up and down in unison. This "electric field" generates the "magnetic field" around it, so the Soul can stay bound to the body. A human child, though born with Full energy, won't survive without help from his parents. A new energy field requires the help of an existing energy field in order to stand on its own.

Rama tried imagining a better way of looking at things. Life is a force, an energy that occurs for reasons not easily comprehensible to a common man. Birth is an energy occurrence on the fabric of Time, in correlation with its related circumstances on the fabric of Space.

Birth circumstances including the time, for the most part, dictate how the life of the energy field is going to be. The son of a Judge becomes a Judge, a daughter of a doctor becomes a doctor, the relative of a Politician becomes a Politician and the same goes for the members of other, not so, sought after walks of life as well.

In an introspective moment, he thinks, where do all the seemingly unfair parts of Life fit in with Rama's, otherwise perfect, thoughts on Life?! He understands fully well that it'll be harsh and cruel to imply that one is facing hardships in life due to a negative karmic balance; and the way they bring the balance close to zero is through reformation.

It would be unwise for the outsiders and third parties to convey the concept of karmic balance. It can create an unfavourable reaction to an uncontrollable and not an instantly curable predicament.

However, when there are no other answers, the subject himself is better off assuming that the uncontrollable entity making his life insufferable is his Karmic balance. To accept the philosophy and make changes required to correct his life trajectory is a good way forward. The Birth Energy seems like it brings with it remnants from its past lives and, to Rama, it made sense that it would. The Big picture of Seven Lives to Salvation suggests that one can't just be good on some occasions that he chooses and not be good on others. Unfortunately, being principled only when it suits you and going back to being a crook all other times, and talking rules when it affects you and breaking them when it doesn't, are too commonplace to even count.

But, when he sees someone who has led an extremely noble life succumbing to a horrible death. Or someone who has done nothing but horrible things in life leading a healthy and happy old age, things will seem like they don't make any sense. That's probably because it's only a small part of the story.

What must one do, upon noticing all these things? It should not be to jump at the chance to correct the wrong, not because correcting the wrong is not the right thing to do, but because treating the symptoms will not cure the disease. Things are rarely what they seem to be on the outside and what's really happening is rarely visible. Peeling off the layers one by one, is the way to get to the core Truth of things. Just like peeling an onion layer by layer, you will arrive at the core of an onion, where there is nothing. That nothing is your goal of karmic balance and in the process attain the Soul maturity needed for Moksha.

Our Inner Energy will guide us in this process. The Energy stays with us, the energy grows and diminishes with us, but who are we? Are we the energy or are we the body? Do we associate more with the soul or the body? The honest answer may also be the wrong one. We are the energy, we are the soul and the body is the custom fitted vehicle to travel in the person dimension for the purpose of progressing on the Soul's path to Moksha.

Birth circumstances and the Birth energy are closely related like a body is to its reflection in the mirror. One of the works that inspired Rama, talks about following one's dreams. It is conveniently ignored that the child is born into a very needy situation. For the child to grow, he needs an environment which is governed by birth circumstances. Birth circumstances have the power to practically govern an individual from his cradle to his grave.

A closer reading of people's dreams might even open a thinker to consider that the dreams we so ardently pursue, are nothing more than conditioning pushed onto the mind by self serving outside interests. Rarely do they have anything to do with the individual himself.

The mere task of overcoming the birth circumstances in each life, can easily account for a couple of lifetimes, in your Soul Maturity and Karmic account balance reduction, 7 lives roadmap. Underestimating or discounting their impact on the individual, only results in additional work in surpassing the disability.

CHAPTER 42

VRATHI

to disconnect

Vrathi is an exercise to train the soul to detach from life, so when time comes, the soul may not struggle. Rama understands that Vrathi is a group activity, generally prescribed to adults. As a part of this exercise, the individual, as a part of a group, is expected to leave all of his family and belongings behind, for a full day once a month. They will be visiting homes of other people; sharing experiences and thoughts with them, while also having the opportunity to learn from their experiences and stories. The exercise ends with resting for the night in the new location.

This is the exact opposite of the popular exercise of proselytising. Vrathi is a self training mechanism, with outside help to train oneself to disconnect from life and all their attachments.

In today's context, when we see someone in their eighties, high on life and full of desires, it's seen as an inspiration. When time comes the soul of this person, having lived a satisfactory life, should not struggle to leave the body. At least that is the idea. What happens when all their desires are not fulfilled, will the soul be happy to let go or will it suffer?

The elders filled with desires is one side of the story; the other side of the same story coin paints a rather disturbing picture. The young generation is maxed out and overwhelmed from the expectations of life. Let's not think for one moment, that the behaviours of the elders and the young ones are unrelated. They have everything to do with each other. The in-between generation having invented all the comforts during their lifetimes, to supposedly improve the quality of life, ended up retrogressing the quality of human beings for all living generations.

When the future generation is no longer interested in their own well being, that's when we have an obligation to declare the official failure of a proper handover of reigns between generations. In the course of the time of a generation, some things improve, some things pass on as they were. Many things take a lot of time to change. To appreciate and accept the time things take, is part of self improvement and a sign of maturity. One of the things that is passed on, is the sacred custody of the sacrosanct Life itself, so it may flourish forever.

The elders have decided to suck the living blood of their young ones, to fulfil their desires. But the young are resisting this unnatural urge on the part of the elders. That is the creation of a Life no one wants to live. The more desires the elders have, the harder the young ones will fall.

Should the young blame their own predecessors for abusing their positional advantage? Should the elders blame the young ones for becoming self aware? The in-between generation has inadvertently broken the chain of communication, resulting in generations unable to understand each other. It was their duty, if possible to improve or, to at least pass on a working communication system.

If they can't even talk to one another, how exactly will they stay connected? The disconnection a.k.a the exercise of Vrathi is not really a challenge, it's more like a chore. Everyone has already become disconnected for a long time. Society has come full circle, unfortunately, in the opposite direction. Instead of working on training themselves to become disconnected, they are starting off their lives by being and staying disconnected.

The more wires that came into the house the less connected we became to one another. Except for the guilt of leaving their loved ones behind helpless, nobody really wants to live. There is nothing worth living for anymore. They are ready to leave the moment they're free from responsibilities. But, that is not the way to go. They must go happily. Not because they're tired or bored or because they've developed an aversion to it.

The young generation has on its hands, the duty of breaking this cycle of madness. Metaphorically speaking, breaking the cycle of building houses nobody wants to buy and then forcing folks to own them. The young generation has on its hands, the duty of building a Life worth living.

CHAPTER 43

RESPECT

more than just people

Rama was done with self-deprecation as his default way of life. To lie and say you are doing well, when you are not, is self-deprecation. You lie, because you believe nobody cares. To discuss with one another and to find solutions for each other, isn't just one way of doing life but the correct one. One hand cleanses the other, just as we help each other. The mind inside the body can't always fathom the reasons for one's suffering, as the reasons can transcend lifetimes. The soul on the other hand knows all. The purpose of life isn't the cleansing of the mind, but of the soul. In order to cleanse one's soul, the mind in the body must also be clean.

For any of the above to happen, the Man must first understand the bedrock of how things work. Character of a person is the foundation and the Respect he gets its mirror image, in this world of mirrors.

To Respect your Parents, Elders and Teachers is taught in school. That's a good thing to teach kids. Respect must also be taught in the contexts beyond people. To respect an opportunity, must be taught; to respect what you have, must be taught; to respect work, both of self and of others must be taught; to respect your circumstances, as they are, must be taught. Because, no matter how discouraging they are - a simple appreciation of the sweat, blood and tears it took, for things to fall in place, builds character; and most importantly, to respect yourself for the right reasons, must be taught. Knowing thyself is a great place to start. Knowing thyself is the righteous path to self respect. It prevents you from respecting yourself for the wrong reasons. Don't respect yourself for the wrong reasons.

One hand cleanses the other, just as we help each other. It may so happen that people require money in order to help you, you have to learn to respect that. Resorting to judgments is only going to drive your potential helper away from you. Evolution has trained us to hide our weaknesses, as a defence mechanism. It will be difficult to determine how desperate people are. You must also respect the desperation, as it is only human nature to react and respond the way people do. All thirsty people have the same experience of dryness down their throats. This is typically when money comes in and starts playing God.

As long as there is no third party that is controlling an individual's ability to help each other, things might still go smoothly. But, when all help across all sectors is governed by third parties, that's when it must be realised that group interests have surpassed the collective interest. You look at your local governance and you see corruption that abound, yet somehow you want to believe that the Governance at higher levels, world over, is full of honest people looking out for the good of Humanity. You prefer to believe people far away from you, while you refuse to extend the same courtesy, for all the right reasons, to those closest to you. It's on us, if we can't see the fallacies in our own intelligence.

To ask for respect is a fool's errand, but you must not be okay with unwarranted disrespect. People's understanding of what commands respect is so out of whack, that any unwarranted and disingenuous respect must be seen as suspect. Money seems to be pretty much the only widely respected commodity. Whoever flashes said commodity gets respect.

The only thing that's your prerogative is the outward respect from you to the world. You give the world respect, for as long as it takes the world to decide to give respect back to you. Your respect to the world on your terms must be timeless and without any expectations. The indignation you may come across in this process is a feature not a flaw. Respect the opportunity to learn about things yet unknown and always respect yourself for being forever introspective.

CHAPTER 44

WANDERLUST

or a Time traveller

In one of the books Rama had read, the author suggests to leave things around as they are and travel. Travelling in and of itself and for all intents and purposes is not a bad thing. But, Travelling as a goal has the potential of being misunderstood. The thing about books or movies and any other romantic mediums of influence, is that they are quite effective in deceptively planting ideas into people's minds.

Imagine a greatly successful newly released book about Travelling and suddenly, a lot of impressionable young readers of this book, have set their life ambitions to become the travellers of the world. I would be remiss if I didn't mention that this particular behaviour of following trends and mirroring personal lives of Celebrities, is the result of heavily utilised marketing strategies.

I would respect a brand that puts the owner's face on the product more than that of an actor or a sportsman. At least then there is an accountability factor that ensures a better quality product. All the money saved from not paying for a famous face, can also be put to benefitting their customers. When you are paying a hefty fee to someone to promote your product, your commitment to the product goes down. Do you want to earn a lot of money or do you want to help a lot of people? This is the question.

In one of the inspiring books, the main character is also questioned about his decision to travel. There was no doubt in Rama's mind that the book he read, although touts itself as fiction, must surely have been influenced by someone's real life. The author using his artistic liberties made the story take turns that would be impossible in real life. Rama could surmise his entire book in few short lines, such as "don't fall for BS" or "there is no such thing as free food", but when competing with colourful imaginations filled with flowery words, hell bent on brainwashing people, he thought it's probably best to have a story and give it a fighting chance.

Travelling or moving away from your place of safety and comfort can be a double-edged sword. Rama is reminded of the story of Ramayana where Sita matha asks God Rama for the Golden deer. God Rama goes after the magical deer to make his beloved wife happy. What wasn't known at the time was that the golden deer was placed there precisely to distract God Rama away from the safety of his home. This resulted in the abduction of Sita matha.

Travel is essential for survival, so to carefully plan one's travel with the needs of self and those closest to you, is a good habit worth exploring. A quick check that can be done here is that of verifying the source of the need for travel. If the Travel need arose from your own mind and there was no subtle implantation of the idea by someone else, such a trip might be important and required on your journey to Moksha. But, if it wasn't, such travel is one more distraction waiting to deflect you away from your path to Moksha.

Rama is also reminded of the Time Travel that was mentioned before. If there was a past decision causing untenable physical travel requirements, it might be worth travelling in time to that moment and undoing that decision.

There must be no doubt that travelling to a new place will bring new stimuli, which will in turn make for an exciting time. Which is why people are always refreshed after returning from a relaxing vacation. The contemporary lifestyle almost dictates that folks take a vacation and travel someplace exotic as a way to relax and decompress. However true it might feel, one must not mistake the excitement or relaxation gained from travel as the solution to their problems. Rama has never felt like he needed to travel. He has always loved what he was doing; he travelled when the occasion called for it, but never on his own volition. To test whether you are one with yourself, try this simple exercise - sit down and be happy.

CHAPTER 45

KNOWING

thyself

One inspiring work says, "to realise thy purpose is the only duty". Rama takes this vague statement and makes it definitive, "to know thyself is the only duty, realising thine purpose is already a subset of knowing thee". You get to know yourself a little better, every time a purpose of yours is realised. There may be a most important or a penultimate purpose in one's life, but there will be innumerable purposes an individual will serve in his journey from Life 1 to Life 7.

Before the head of the reader starts to spin, Rama wants to end this thought by saying that all these purposes are, are opportunities to know yourself, on your way to realising the ultimate purpose, which is the attainment of Moksha.

In the early lives, you have to do things in order to know, but as Lives go on, doing comes easy, but knowing becomes difficult. You have already plucked all the low hanging fruit, so to speak. Now, it's the turn to go after the really tough lessons. People succumb to inertia and get so lost in doing, they lose track of the task of the all important Knowing. Small adjustments to our routine may help address this gap.

We are wired to observe. We observe everything and everyone because observation gives us intelligence that can prove helpful. How a person conducts himself, the presentation, the communication, etc., speak volumes more than what the person himself may be able to tell you about himself. So, when someone says, just ask people for the truth, and you follow their advice, you're venturing into territories the person of interest himself may not know.

Take an example of a household where a husband always talks about how expensive things have become. Even though it may not have been his intention, he will have indirectly conveyed to his wife to reduce household expenditure. And when a wife or a husband dreads about how difficult or expensive it is to raise a child, it is automatically conveyed that having another child may not be in the best interest of that household.

On the same lines, the way you conduct yourselves speaks volumes more than words you use to convey your side of the story. Just as you observe others, you must train yourselves to observe yourself. Observe the changes in behaviour with changes in ambience, the mood swings, the pleasantness and the annoyances. Observing your own conduct will help you know yourself. Until you are a master of who you are, you will be predisposed to becoming a slave of someone else.

Thus far, it was you helping yourself, to know yourself, by observing yourself. There are other forces that want you to succeed. These are typically the family, friends, teachers, followers and the Universe. These external forces assist you with messages, innuendo and omens.

Understanding the predicament of honest people, who get dinged for following what was taught as a virtuous way of life, will help you understand the complex nature of the setup one has to deal with.

In repeating and reporting what you saw exactly as you saw, without fully comprehending the size and scale of the matter, you may be serving a self interest of another. You are simply falling into an elaborate trap, laid out to identify the suckers. What if it isn't your role to simply report your findings but to act on your findings?! And, when you find out that you are not permitted to do so, would you still be willing to be an obedient reporter?! What if you were never designed to follow orders, but were meant to follow your Heart?!

Who are you? The Outside World sees you in the roles you perform. A child, a grandchild, a parent, a grandparent, a doctor, a lawyer, an engineer, etc. A role that is often ignored is the role of a spouse. Conventional wisdom suggests that the relationship between a wife and a husband is between themselves and no third party interference is advisable. The prevailing understanding that marriage is a relationship between equals creates confusion because abilities of no two persons are the same. If two persons were of exactly the same abilities, what would be the point of a union.

In a humble submission, Rama suggests that marriage is a union of unequals. Inequality is an important reason for the union. Marriage is the thread that binds the 2 unequal beads that come together to become a perfect unit. One's imperfections are covered by the other's exceptionalism in making up for the shortcomings of the others. If men and women were equal the institution of marriage wouldn't have been possible.

In his endeavour of knowing himself, Rama observed that the most important tool he had was self discipline. You can't know yourself if you are not observant, vigilant and disciplined. The person is expected to be extremely careful with his time management. This is because there are several other people and things he is responsible for, answerable and accountable to. It's possible that you might forget about other things in the spirit of the moment that consumes you. This is where one receives the help of the universe in the form of omens. Obey the omens. Even if they are not immediately useful, keep the lessons for future use. It's very possible that major disasters can be averted, as long as those who are responsible, take action in the nick of time.

Another observation Rama wants to document, in this exercise of self discovery, is that of his consistent nature. Rama has changed careers, as and when he realised that they didn't suit him. He has seen in his previous careers, how those with flexible personal ethics and questionable integrity have gone on to build impressive wealth portfolios. He is seeing the same thing repeat in his latest career as well.

To use an old phrase, "you can take someone out of the city, but you can't take the city out of them". Rama changing careers did not mean he was ready to build wealth by bending himself. One could argue that the reason he had to change careers was because he couldn't compromise on his principles.

The old adage goes, "Fool me once, shame on you; Fool me twice, shame on me", to which Rama adds, "but, if I exist to be fooled every time, I'm hopeless. In other words, it's my nature to be fooled". Each has their own reasons they tell themselves and some are bigger fools than others. First they get fooled, then they go hunting for reasons justifying why they were fooled. It's okay to be fooled and even okay to be a forever fool, as long as you are not the one fooling yourself. If you cannot know yourself, at the very least, don't lie to yourself. It's practically the lowest of things you can do.

One of Rama's friends at a young age told him that at the time of sleeping, he always covers himself head to toe. It was a practice he held very dear, so much so that he wouldn't fall asleep if he hadn't fully covered himself with the blanket. Then one day he read a book which explained the proper way to sleep, it suggested not to cover the face as it might be harmful. Overnight, Rama's friend changed his sleeping habit and stopped covering his head under the blanket. His long term practice didn't mean much if it was harmful to him. Because more than the practice or the blanket, he respects himself, and his longtime habit stood no chance before the responsibility and bearing he had on himself.

Finally, in the interactions that occur in the course of our lives and earning a livelihood, it's a simplified form of contributing to each other in the form of whatever they are good at doing. Unfortunately, someone being good at something is not always a guarantee that the proceeds from his work are good enough to pay for his needs. This explains the price variation for various goods and services, supposedly dependent on supply and demand. The failure to realise the ominous role of advertising hand-in-hand with manufactured demand, can turn the tables on anything at any time.

Take an example of a country that suffers from high rates of a particular illness. For whatever reason the price for the treatment of this illness is unaffordable. Therefore, people simply don't seek the treatment and leave themselves to the mercy of Gods. It's not exactly a good Country to be in. That is one explanation, but that's not an option. Some people don't realise this predicament until it's too late. Also, people can't simply wake up and leave their country.

There are personal principles and there are universal principles. In the pursuit of knowing thyself, we are expected to learn both. One of the universal principles is that Patience is a virtue. Things will turn in the favour of the Righteous. The delay you may experience is because the Universe is waiting for you to be fully prepared and in parallel it is placing everything in place for your turn. In all these learnings, you know yourself.

There should be no greater goal than to know thyself. Once you know yourself, you turn from merely being a last line of defence to your own cause, to becoming a front line warrior, preserver and protector of everything you consider dear.

Rama acknowledges that he may never cross what wasn't achieved by his predecessors. Because the weight of evolution that forged him into this being, shall weigh heavily when he forgets where he came from. It would all be for nothing when he's sprinting in a path that is starkly in contrast with everything his predecessors have steadfastly worked toward. In adamantly continuing to do so, Rama, of all the people might end up becoming the inevitable stumbling block in his own oath.

The sacred pursuit of knowing thyself includes the equally sacred pursuit of knowing thy family history, going back as long back as it is practically possible. Studying the lives, lifestyles, successes, failures, and the recurring patterns of behaviour among the members of the family tree, can provide invaluable insights into genuine and unfiltered reasons behind your own style of thinking and being.

All the unnecessary commotion from the lack of this understanding about overcoming one's own nature, has caused Rama a lot of pain. To impose an expectation on the child, without considering that the child may never overcome what his father and grandfathers have not achieved, might break him. The child as his prerogative may choose to achieve this never before achieved, very difficult goal. Such a journey is perhaps the manifestation of human Evolution. The help of all the ingredients, both positive and negative, can bring about the magical potion that makes the goal possible.

When you are consumed by something for a long period of time, it's no longer about the superficiality of the main story. It becomes about so many short stories that come carefully weaved together. The message each one of those conveys and convinces you to walk away from your own fractured reality.

You are so deep into it, that you are conducting the catharsis with passion. Not because the main story is less important but because the main story has already become more important than your own story. You are unable to forgive yourself for being carried away. You want to understand why something so sweet and beautiful has become so instrumental in distracting you from your Kartavyam.

Chapter 46
WRITING

to correct the wrongs

No one should write, because it's their pastime, because what's written can't be destroyed. The word Akshar literally translates to, one that can't be destroyed. Therefore, filling up our forever storage vault with fluff may not be a good idea. If it were a long time ago when there were not enough books, the prevalent attitude may have slightly wavered in favour of more books. But, writing of books or more broadly, creation of content cannot be purely for entertainment. The world has way too many distractions as it is, and these are causing irreparable damage to billions of lives, as we speak.

Rama considers this work as the greatest rewriting of the biggest lies ever published. To say the right thing and do the wrong thing and when questioned, say the right thing and do the wrong thing again, has become the modus operandi. We deserve what we get, because we are not smart enough to figure out the con. Duplicity is the name of the game.

One thing that's obvious in our Nature, is that we're suckers for a good story. Adding to which, it's also evident that storytelling is perhaps our greatest strength. According to Rama, it's the single biggest reason behind how we were able to preserve rich cultural traditions and pass on the wisdom of Life since time immemorial. With so much history with storytelling, came a weakness. Falling hard for Stories has become our weakness. Con-artists have figured out this weakness and started selling contraband in the form of stories.

When people start waking up to this scam, the "freedom" fighters start to emerge from the woodworks, making sanctimonious claims. Phrases like "it being a free country" and "nobody held a gun to the head" are used to justify. They say, "what was being done was purely an exercise of the right to freedom of life and that both parties were willing participants in whatever damage may have occurred".

"If you don't like a book, don't buy it", say those who are incharge, in their vehement defence of the Right to Free Speech. We are supposed to go on with our lives, as if it's a free and fair marketplace, suggesting that the buyers have to make choices wisely. In the contemporary world, the case with the books can be well illustrated instead by taking the example of the movies.

The budgets for the marketing of movies are equal to, if not more than the budgets of the making of the movies. What does it say? It says that there are brilliant minds behind closed doors that are working very hard at selling you the movie than there are minds making the movie. The marketing begins before the movie does, to say nothing of the enticement of the audiences with item songs and catchy dance numbers in skimpy clothing.

People will take advantage of people's proclivities to sell whatever they are selling. They'll sell first and discuss the ethics of it later, at the lavish dinners funded by the profits from the very same sale. When questioned on a public stage about damage being done, those who are incharge will play dumb. It'll be said that that was never their intention. There may not be a single movie that doesn't resort to shortcuts for the sake of the wow factor.

The protagonist is most likely a smuggler, liar, cheater or all of the above, which he won't be in the last minute of the movie. But throughout the movie, he's a violence prone, drug addict, drunkard, criminal who is most definitely not an upstanding citizen. When asked about civic duty, the makers renege on promises with excuses and relinquish any personal responsibility. It will be said that they are an industry in the business of making money, then they go and conveniently take cover behind the fine print of the contracts, indemnification clauses and disclaimers such as smoking kills and alcohol being injurious.

A competition between unequals is not a competition, it's a bloodbath. A typical moviegoer who has been primed to follow the trend becomes gullible and ends up falling prey to the propaganda. A common man is no match to the elaborate and profound capabilities of movie production houses. So, when those incharge say that if you don't like a book, don't buy it, it's an oversimplification of a very grave problem that our society faces. Taking the example of movies helps in explaining the problem. Books are the foundation on which the movies are built on, so the argument about the money and marketing will stand true on its own merits to whomever wants to dig a little deeper.

Which is why Rama is taking a note of all the various ways he can be distracted. He is also making note of all the ways he can avoid becoming distracted. Kartavyam is generally spoken in terms of the duty of a soldier, with respect to the protection of the peace, stability, integrity and the preservation of the way of life of a Nation. Although, the duty of the individual is less significant than what a soldier does for the protection of his motherland, the individual's Kartavyam of attaining Moksha is not far behind.

Soldiers protecting our borders are the single most important entity enabling the citizens to pursue their Kartavyams in peace. Rama would be remiss if he didn't acknowledge the soldiers within the borders, the heroes in daily life, the scientists, teachers, doctors, engineers and all those men and women who are making the lives of citizens of Bharat better at the expense of their own. In spite of all the theories Rama may have documented, he strongly believes that those soldiers who sacrificed themselves for the sake of their nation have certainly attained Moksha for their selfless way of Life.

In Rama's story, "each and every one is a hero", is not just some cliche thrown out to make the reader feel better, but it also happens to be the most effective way to go about and handle Life. When everyone thinks they are a hero, they solve their problems themselves independently and even try to help others when possible. This scenario is much better than, when no one feels like they are a hero and end up depending on someone else for help.

CHAPTER 47

ENSLAVEMENT

in its many forms

Where the greatest enslavement tool ever invented is sold as the path of empowerment; Where the Nation state, the protector and guarantor of the freedom and liberty of its citizens, is bought and sold by the slave owners perpetrating the greatest crime of oppression, subjugation in the name of democracy - The mockery of the beliefs bestowed upon us as virtues, has become a useful tool, in the wrong hands, to mould and extract desired behaviour.

The constructs of society are walls of the prison preventing you from escaping into the truth. Luckily, you are never too far from the truth even if you feel that you are a lost cause. That is, because you, in all your purity of existence, are the truth. You are the Truth and no one can change that. But attempts may be made to try and waste your life, so be vigilant.

After the long journey of this life, you may come back yet again in another life in the pursuit of yourself, several times over until you find yourself, which is your Truth, which is nothing but your pursuit of Moksha.

Enslavement coming in the form of empowerment and empowerment coming in the form of living a slave life with limited means, is confusing to the most brilliant of minds. Enslavement of the mind by an outsider is quite different from the endurance of self created pain and suffering on your own path to freeing your mind.

Enslavement in its most common form occurs in a series of small instalments, in order to avoid detection. It starts with the abuse of one's favourable standing with another, in an unfair exercise of powers or more commonly as a betrayal of one's trust. It's not as if, when you find out how enslavement occurs, you are ready to fight against it. Contrary to conventional wisdom, where people are expected to resist outside control as an infringement over their autonomy, most of us are volunteering ourselves away to the sophistication of modern day slavery.

To get a glimpse of the level of sophistication, you may ask the question of, what came first?

Did the plan to build an evil empire come first and then the technology that is enabling it, was made possible? Or, did technology come first and then came the plan to build an evil empire? The latter is probably understandable. Taking advantage of the opportunities to enrich oneself at the expense of others, though not noble, is understandable. But, if it's the former, we better run for the hills because there's nothing scarier. What else could be coming out of the box next?

The next time we are logging in into our free-to-use cloud accounts that we are pouring ourselves into, just ask yourself this question - which came first - and then go back to doing whatever you are doing. It's not like we have much of a choice. At least this way things will become interesting, if only for a few minutes, in an otherwise predictable life of a modern day slave.

It should not be about pointing fingers. There must be a warranted introspection - Are we a slave to ourselves, are we slaves to our families, are we slaves to our society and our country or is there another angle?

Are we slaves to a lifestyle that has developed an affinity to want shiny new things to flaunt, as a symptom of the shallowness we so dearly espouse? or are we simply slaves by inheritance of the lives and habits of our parents, which force us into inherited slavery?

So many questions, but never any time to sit down and figure things out, thought Rama.

Why are all these people running around so busily? and why are there so many problems plaguing the society? Let's not be remiss and think that these questions are causing each other. They are, for the promise of the most sacred pledges of the world, exactly one and the same thing.

Yet another question to answer the reasons for enslavement, is whether we were grandfathered into these sneaky enslavement contracts. Contracts where the consideration doubly helps the lender and ties down the borrower with a debt that's impossible to pay off. Forever rising inflation is an effective lowering of wages.

The turning of the page to a future history of 21st century emancipation proclamation moment seems improbable, but we can't lose hope. We are fully equipped to solve this problem with the back of our hand. All these problems are in fact only one problem and therefore need only one solution - being true to ourselves.

Rama will be the first to accept that it is not always clear what it means to be true to oneself. When faced with such situations, Rama recites his mantra with total conviction. "When you don't know what to do, fight for what you believe". He also reminds himself of the fail safe for this mantra - "Just don't let your beliefs be dictated by somebody else".

A classic example of a grandfathered-in contracts would be, when the Colonizers would add to the debt, all money spent on laying the Railways. Because these tracks were laid on our land on their watch. The colony people never stood a chance! The citizens are shown justification that we ought to pay these amounts back with interest. The double loss occurs in this way. These tracks that were laid all across were done so not on the insistence of the public as a means of public transportation. These were laid primarily to loot the nation of all its natural resources, food produce and precious metal wealth accumulated by the kingdoms over thousands of years.

One might argue that we are paying the heavy price for the open and welcoming attitude of our predecessors. The innate national philosophies that served the world for thousands of years - vasudhaika kutumbam and athithi devo bhava - have become the most abused loopholes of the past thousand years. Things can't be maintained in a healthy balance when the daily rule becomes - all my money is my money and all your money is our money.

Which brings to the fore, the moment of a National introspection with respect to the updation and improvement of our National principles and philosophies. We finally go ahead with the upgradation of National Policy to the modern times, where each is forced to face the reality or pay the price for casually shrugging off any and all accountability.

No one can enslave the one who is self aware.   Self awareness is the definition of Freedom.

CHAPTER 48

IT IS OKAY

to fail

Life is not just about following your dreams, but it's about being okay to fail. Not just Love, but all unadulterated pure emotions are all languages of the world. It's our job to understand what they want to tell us and why.

When you really want something it's not because the desire is from the soul of the Universe. The Universe does not have a desire from us, nor do we from the Universe. Everything happens because a piece of the Super Soul, Paramatma, breaks away and starting from that moment of separation works ever so hard to become whole again. Like when a member of a family drifts apart and he wants to rejoin his family, so he can become whole once again. "The purpose of the whole exercise may elude me now, but I'll find out", thought Rama.

It is somewhat similar to how the cells of the organs of the body die off and new cells take their place, and within some time the whole body is regenerated with new cells. Perhaps this, breaking away and reunification, is also a part of the process of rejuvenation of the Paramatma himself, as it aids in the goal of perfecting the Super Soul. Rama acknowledges that he is too small to speak about the matters he is opining about. It's his desperate act of devotion to Life that he so passionately observes.

To those who are curious about the phenomenon, this is the story about time travel where consciousness travels through time without actually feeling it.

"Whatever the reason may be, why does it have to be so difficult ?", sighed Rama. "It's only difficult because we make it", thought Rama. We can make things difficult for us, that's a given, and we also make things difficult for others. We do this because we are petty. If someone is doing better than us, we burn with jealousy. Which makes for an uneven level playing field because there will always be more people motivated to work against you, than those inclined to work in your favour. The rules of this game are unfair.

People gang up in groups in order to subvert the aspirations of others, even when they have no connection with the real aggressors. You are expected to bring your fight in the open, while you are being attacked in the darkness of the night. It is no wonder people switch to the other side the first chance they get. They are smart in the short term for doing so, but also stupid in the long term for not seeing the big picture. A setup such as this is precisely why it's okay to fail.

Most of us will fail, but, on our side is fate. Which is why we are given 7 chances. We are not just given the chances so we can fail, but to learn. When it's time for us to rejoin the Paramatma, we take with us all we learn.

What is your first reaction when you walk into the world and you face a cent percent chance of defeat? Is it of disappointment or anger or complete loss of all hope or of an increased commitment to become better? "Try not to take yourself and others too seriously", Rama tells himself. There is no need to become apprehensive. The attitude must be one of readiness to take on whatever may come. You must fear only yourselves of becoming incapable of action when times come calling.

One of the natural urges is to act on every little thing at the outset and end up exhausting ourselves. Sometimes, the approach must be one of achieving the most effective immediate outcome in the shortest amount of time, with a solid plan in place for the most comprehensive outcome. Let's take an example of loud noises in your neighbourhood. In an ideal world, people don't blast loud noises and they don't cast an evil eye at other people's happiness, but, our World is not ideal, it's real.

We're on it on our personal journey to Moksha, not to discipline other people. Instead of trying to shut every source of loud sound as an immediate measure and in the process lose your mind, it's best to start with purchasing high quality ear plugs. Just like that, instead of trying to source all your happiness from material things, you can make a fraction of the effort and try finding happiness inside yourselves.

We must live wisely, otherwise risk losing interest in life. You are your last line of defence, but you are also the only line of defence of your children. In your case, you may choose to give up, but in the case of your children, you must not make a choice. Because when you don't protect, they too will lose interest in life. Life lesson alert! In protecting the children you protect Life itself.

The cycle of perpetuating lives-that-have-lost-interest-in-life must be broken. "Make life on Earth worth living", thought Rama. From the way things are, it's clear that we all have lives, but lack the interest. It is nobody's job to tell others this, but he says it out loud, not for the sake of others but for the sake of himself, "don't contribute to your own loss of interest in life". When faced with adversity, one must remember that there are at least 2 ways to solve a problem. One with outside help and the other with inside help. There won't be many problems to which you can't find the answers inside. Training to use the answers inside, also trains you for Moksha.

A Home is not four walls and a Family is not just a bunch of people clubbed together. All those children and parents who are physically falling apart, in the process of raising their children well and taking care of their parents, are well advised to do so. What else are they going to do with their bodies, when they are dead?! A family home is a child care centre, an old age home and a highly motivated Innovation and solution studio, all at the same time. It's an all encompassing, self sustaining, microcosm of the larger society that it's a part of.

As its core function, a family, to the outside of itself, is to communicate and mingle with others. Which opens it up for infection but also creates the chance of becoming the cure to the ailments infesting the other family units. Because of our in-built mirroring mechanism, the family only needs to be true to itself and fight for what it believes. Seeing which, others will gain inspiration and motivation to do the same. It may not be the exact same as what the inspiring family was doing, but same in the sense of being true to themselves and fighting for what they believe. Some will succeed and some will fail, but in this process Life itself will have gained the interest to carry on.

It's okay to fail, because Family is always on standby to catch us when we fall.

CHAPTER 49

THE ANTIDOTE

to Noise

Antidote to the hundreds of crores of people affected by the incorrect application of half knowledge, like watching a short video and embarking on a mission to outer space, is to bust the myth that you can change your destiny. The destiny is, was and will always be Moksha. In Moksha, we find our shared destiny. This conviction is the antidote for those who have to live in the physical world, away from the chemical influence of ideas that "want" to change the world.

How we are perceived by others is not in our control. There are too many others and only one you - it's practically impossible to control. Your focus on how others perceive you is precisely the noise you must avoid. When others disapprove of you for reasons they themselves may not fully comprehend, that is on them.

They do not yet realise that you are not their enemy, in fact they fail to see the basic point that there are no enemies. They can't even process that their disapproval of you, or of anyone else is of little consequence to you, to themselves or to the world. Rama recites this mantra to himself, "there are no enemies, there is only you".

Rama can feel that his thoughts have reached a logical end point in this exercise of voicing his thoughts on books that inspired him. He wants to add a few things that are worthwhile.

The work ethic of those who suffer, should be that others should not suffer. It should not be that all others must suffer too. Because such an attitude is sure to make the whole world miserable. The attitude fix for this potential problem is to inculcate the virtue of mercy.

When the whole world starts its judgement based on the Job you do, and this job cannot include efforts on family, it becomes the only source of respect. For decades now, Fathers have become material providers only, with almost no meaningful contributions to the family. The desperate current state of the family unit is the price being paid for this decades long neglect.

We are already AI, when what we are doing is not an original idea. The only difference is that Human AI is far less lethal, as it is in a distributed form. The creation and development of a computer AI will first concentrate and then amplify this stupidity of unoriginal ideas. The past saying on this matter that says, the only way to win against AI is not to fight, is incorrect. You can't win with AI. The only way to survive is to not fight. To win is a different ballgame. Something so seemingly harmless as engaging in a conversation or doing "getting to know AI" exercises can easily be traps that land you in dangerous predicaments.

The only way we can ensure that AI doesn't destroy mankind is by hardwiring into its circuitry the ethos of Mercy. "The job of AI is to show Mercy". It almost sounds like the job description of God. Can we create God? Gods created thus far have given a lot of history for us to learn from, so let's at least aim to not repeat the mistakes.

There are no enemies, there is only you. Almost every horrible thing that happened in the world can be shown to have roots in the actions of the victims. Let's not be enthusiastic about handing over the power over us to unknown entities. It should not be that complicated to grow your own food and prepare yourself a healthy meal. Do we really need algorithms sifting and probing through our every waking thought and "suggest" to us "what we may like" ?!

 The Anti-dote to noise is the clarity of your thoughts. Don't be carried away by outside influences, because you feel like you only know a little. Most of what's out there is garbage anyway, so knowing only a little can only become your strength. Use it! You must use yourself and all you have to become free. Being free allows you to pursue your path to Moksha. To attain Moksha is your Kartavyam.

Rama arrived at the final parallel needed to be drawn between the Internal world and the External world, vis-a-vis, the Biological and the Physical worlds. When something hits the body and it hurts, what is the first reaction? The closest hand goes to it and presses the part that's hurting and somehow a slight relief sets in. What happens when someone in the external world, i.e., the physical world is hurting? Those closest to the person go to him and console him, and just like in the internal world, a slight relief sets in.

Rama understands this behaviour as the coming together of the good cells (persons), i.e., the healthy cells, i.e., the unhurt cells inside the body to the cell (person) that's hurting and share with it their health and help with the healing process. Since, there will always be more unhurt cells (persons) in the body (society), the self healing starts occurring right away. In the off chance that there are more hurt cells than there are healthy cells, it means that the last healthy cell will have to fight till its last joule of energy to make more healthy cells. Because, the survival of the body depends on the survival of the cell. Just like that, the survival of the external world depends on the survival of the internal world.

Blaming the unhealthy cells or hurt persons for the decay of our society, is like blaming the Chameleon for changing colours. Don't blame the Chameleon, blame the predatory nature of its circumstances for making it change its Nature.

Rama strongly believes that every last unhurt person, driven by the desire to fulfil his Kartavyam of attaining Moksha, must also fight for the survival of the Society. Because, without a living Society there can be no Moksha for anyone.

Rama completes his 7th Life and attains Moksha.